Dante and Me

A Journey

for Joyce
from Betsy

Enjoy!

June 2009

Pace e bene

Dante and Me

A Journey

Betsy Jordan

With illustrations by Nancy Haver

HISTORICAL DISCLAIMER

Although I include some general truths about the fourteenth century in Italy, some characters and events are real and others are fictitious. My goal has been to recreate the spirit of Dante's time, rather than to replicate historical events.

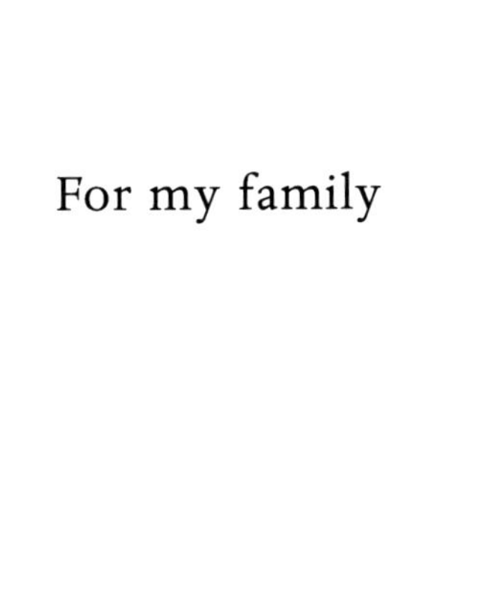

For my family

INTRODUCTION

Who was Dante?

The chiseled dark face with the hook-nosed profile below the laurel wreath looks out at us from Italian medals and paintings. The body, although covered with a long robe, seems taut and muscular. His jaw is set; he appears resolute and serious.

In 1265 in Florence, the city of flowers, a baby was born named Dante Alighieri. Recorded details are sparse, but we know that his father was Alighiero II, of a noble family well known in the city. The birth probably occurred in May. Young Dante grew up to be a civic leader and an author, writing political treatises as well as poetry. His most famous poem, the *Commedia* or *Divine Comedy*, traces a journey through the afterlife to Hell (*Inferno*), Purgatory (*Purgatorio*), and Heaven (*Paradiso*). Due to political infighting, he was exiled from Florence in 1302 and spent the rest of his life in exile. Dante died in Ravenna in 1321.

Lake Garda
Sirmione
Peschiera
Vicenza
Verona
Venice
Padua
Mantua
Parma
Adriatic Sea
Ravenna
LUNIGIANA
Camaldoli
Lucca
Florence
Poppi
CASENTINO
San Gimignano
Siena
Assisi
Sant'Antimo
Rome

CHAPTER ONE

I tried to be a good father to the lambs and goats *Zia* Bianca left under my care, since I didn't have a father and mother of my own any more. *Zia* Bianca's kitchen was warm and Massimo and Antonio welcomed me as their brother, but the hole in my heart never entirely closed. It shrank, though, when we took the animals to the upper pastures in the early summer. Then, I was the papa, and the lambs and goats clambered after me. At night in the mountains, they curled up close to me and I could feel their hearts beating and touch their soft fur. They whispered to me in goat language and nuzzled the warm places under my arms. I felt loved again.

"Benito, get up quickly!" Massimo shouted from *Zia* Bianca's kitchen toward my hut in the trees behind the cottage. "Today we take the goats and sheep to the high pastures! Mama has a bowl of porridge for you in the kitchen."

I jumped up, folding my straw pallet and pulling my brown tunic over my head. The early morning sun streamed through my window, forming a gold circle on the floor where I had been sleeping.

"Let's start now!" I called to Massimo and Antonio. I gulped down the porridge and asked *Zia* Bianca for some of her hearth bread to take in our packs, along with warm milk in our wineskins. We could eat more breakfast along the way.

Waiting for springtime in the Casentino had taken forever. I loved the hilly farmland around my aunt's house, but the upper pastures were like a dream: rolling green meadows, rocky outcroppings, caves to play in, and butterflies to chase. The goats and sheep could climb wherever they wanted, and so could we. My cousins Massimo and Antonio and I tended the animals and ate sheep and goat cheese along with the bread and fruit that *Zia* Bianca sent up every few days. When we played tunes on the flutes we carved from hollow sticks, the notes echoed far away, bouncing back to us from the nearby peaks. We slept either in the open air under a canopy of stars, wrapped in our warm sheepskins, or in the summer cabin. To reach the loft we climbed a wooden ladder, and as we lay in the sweet smelling heaps of warm hay we could hear the tinkling of the bells we hung from leather straps around the necks of our lambs and kids. In the evening, after we had milked the goats and ewes and secured all the animals in pens of vines and bark, we lay on our backs in the deep grass watching the clouds and the moon. That was our favorite story-telling time. We told stories in the fall and winter, too, down at *Zia* Bianca's in the Casentino, but up here our stories were larger than life. Massimo was the best story teller.

"Massimo, tell me about the wizard who paints the leaves red and orange in the autumn. How does he disappear with the first frost, when his cousin the snow *strega* takes his place?"

"Benito," he said, "that icy witch, the *strega*, floats down from the coldest peaks. She whitens the world with her wand and shrivels the leaves. But her life is short, because when the streams begin to run again in the spring she turns to water and dashes down these valleys to join her friends the river gods. Then they all go together, the snow witch, the leaf painting wizard, and the river gods, to make their way toward the Arno River and then to the ocean."

I liked imagining her with wings of spun ice, hovering as she sprinkled snowflakes. But in the mornings we had work to do, so I went to sleep dreaming of witches and wizards and river gods. When the sun rose behind the mountains I washed the milk pots in the creek and turned the wheels of drying cheese. The fermenting curds smelled salty.

"Lead the babies to the smaller high meadows today, Benito. Antonio and I will take the big flocks to the west pastures."

"Come with papa," I said to my charges, "today we're climbing up toward where the *strega* and the wizard live." The path zigzagged, and the goats and sheep jostled one another. Some of the bigger babies took the lead, shoving the smaller ones out of the way. I guess they thought they knew the way better than I did! Once we reached the high flat lands, the animals and I were alone with the world except for the birds and the grasshoppers. Up here I was king.

"*Olà, pecorina*," I said to the smallest sheep. "Watch where you go exploring today." Or, "Stay back from the rim of the ledge, *capretto*." They baa'd and bleated in response, looking up at me with big warm eyes.

I knew the craggy rocks held danger, but I couldn't stay away from them. What treasure might be hiding there? Once I had caught a glimpse of a snake, not as long as I was tall, but with a handsome diamond-shaped head. *Zia* Bianca told me later that its fangs were poisonous, but I wanted to see it again up close. It had scurried off into a crack in the rocks before I could get a good look. Or maybe I would find a wild boar, the kind of *cinghiale* people hunted for savory meat. But so far all I had found were rabbits, sometimes a porcupine, lots of beetles, and now and then a stinging scorpion.

This day I couldn't resist venturing farther up, into the area where the sloping pastureland gave way to sharp boulders and scrub oak. The bravest of the goats followed me, since their hooves could cling to rocks. Seeing us scramble higher, the lambs huddled together below, baa-ing and shaking their heads so their bells rang louder and louder.

My favorite little goat was the one I called *Papaverito* after the bright red poppies through which we had walked as we climbed through the lower fields on our way to the mountains. "*Papaverito,* stay close!" I shouted, but just as I spoke he leapt up to a narrow ledge and dashed to the west, toward a stony crag. I lunged for him, scraping my knees until they bled, but he was just beyond my reach. My body shook and I fell, scrambling to get back on my feet, just as I saw a sharp-fanged snake dart out of a crack in front of *Papaverito*. The little goat, enjoying his new freedom and practicing his jumping skills, paid no attention until the snake's forked tongue lashed out into *Papaverito*'s leg.

"Ahi!" I cried out. He whimpered and stumbled to his knees as I scrambled to him. The snake's fangs were still darting in and out, but I thought only of my beloved *Papaverito* as I scooped up his tiny body. Scooting and half sliding down the slope, I called to the other goats to follow. "*Sbrigati*," I called, "we must hurry to get *Papaverito* down to the cabin." Massimo and Antonio heard us coming and saw my torn clothes and my bleeding knees. "*Dio mio*, Benito? What happened to you and *Papaverito*?"

"A snake bit him and I think he will die! Look, he is panting and crying!"

Taking out a knife from his belt, Massimo cut a gash above the snake bite on *Papaverito*'s leg. Already the flesh around the wound was swelling and turning an ugly bloody red. Massimo put his mouth to the cut and began sucking out the venom, spitting it out each time and rinsing his mouth with goat's milk from Antonio's wineskin.

Before long *Papaverito* stopped trembling and Massimo laid him down, covering him with warm hay. "He will live, Benito, but don't ever take the animals higher than the flat pastures again. The goats can't understand the dangers in these mountains, and it's our job to keep them safe and healthy. What will *Zia* Bianca think?"

"Do you have to tell her about it, Massimo? I only wanted to explore." My heart sank as the words pushed out of my mouth.

"She needs to know, Benito. We are responsible for her flock."

My heart was pounding like a wild boar and my eyes reddened with tears. "*Ahimè*, Massimo. To think that *Papaverito* could have died because of me! You too could have died, sucking out the venom."

"My father taught me how to do that to save my own life, or my brother's or yours, if one of us surprised a snake."

"*Grazie*, Massimo, *tante grazie.*"

That night I didn't play my flute, and the stars didn't look as bright to me as they had before. I thought about what I had done. The next day I kept my lambs and baby goats close to me, and sang to them as we walked to the flat meadows. A hawk circled above, cawing noisily, and I looked up toward the crags without any desire to go exploring again. I sat down in the grass and cradled some of my faithful charges. "Ah, *bambini*," I said to them, "here is tender grass, along with some dandelions and wild mustard, and the creek water is cool and refreshing. Stay with me." They clustered about me and *Papaverito* put his soft pointed nose in my lap. I was happy once again, but I had no way of knowing that hiking in the Casentino mountains and facing danger would soon become a central part of my life.

CHAPTER TWO

I first met Master Dante when he came to my village in the Casentino. Massimo and Antonio knew of him, because Dante's family owned lands in Pagnolle nearby, and he came up to our country hills from time to time to check on his tenants and to collect rent. The last time he came I had been up in the summer pastures shepherding my sheep and goats, but one day in early fall he came by *Zia* Bianca's cottage after I had returned. I was out in the back garden pulling weeds so that our turnips and potatoes would yield a healthy harvest that fall, but I heard his children laughing and scurried to the front door.

"*Buon giorno*, son. I am Dante Alighieri, and these are my children, Giovanni, Iacopo, Pietro, and Antonia. They will be staying with you and Massimo and Antonio this afternoon while I make the rounds visiting my farmers." How happy I was to meet them! The boys were older, near the ages of my cousins, but Antonia was not much bigger than I.

"Hurry," I said, "the sun is still high in the sky and we have all afternoon to play and explore. I will finish the turnip-weeding tomorrow."

The first thing I did was hang a rope swing from the barn door so Giovanni and I could hide in the hayloft above and swoop down to startle the horses when they came in. Pietro and Iacopo were our guards, telling us when the horses were coming, and Antonia piled up hay beneath the door so we could land in a heap without hurting ourselves if the rope broke. Massimo and Antonio pretended to be horses before the real ones came back. Their neighs sounded believable, but no matter how hard they stamped their feet they couldn't make as much noise as our farm animals. As the afternoon wore on we all got hungry, so we went home to see if my aunt could give us some goat cheese and apples.

Before Ser Dante returned we sat on the packed earth floor, eating our cheese and apples and talking. His children spoke of life in Florence, the city to the south and west of the Casentino, down in the valley of the Arno River. My eyes widened as I listened. I had never been to the city and could only imagine what it would be like. Like us, they had daily chores to do, but their work was very different from ours in the mountains. When they said they were responsible for tidying the books, I didn't understand.

"Books!" I exclaimed. "I have seen one in our church at the corner of the square. The Father there reads from it on Sundays." *Zia* Bianca had no books in her house, and neither she nor Massimo nor Antonio nor I knew how to read.

Giovanni spoke up. "Our father loves books and reads to us often. Papa tells us how he learned to love books when he was a boy."

"What is so wonderful about a book?" I asked.

"I like them because their leather covers smell warm and oily, like sheep. And Papa says that because he was careful, his papa and our step-grandmother— after our grandmother Bella died, he married Lapa—let him carry books around with him in his knapsack. He especially liked reading in quiet places, where he could curl up and bury himself in words and stories."

I thought of burying myself in *Papaverito*'s soft fur, or how Massimo and Antonio and I buried ourselves in the soft hay in the summer cabin's loft, after a day of working outdoors. But how could you bury yourself in a book? I was full of questions.

"I think books smell like the warm embers in the fire after Lapa finishes cooking," Antonia added. "Papa says the parchment pages are made from sheepskin. To make leather binding from sheepskins takes a long time, curing the soft skins and removing all the bristles and fur."

"I know sheepskins for sleeping, because Massimo and Antonio and I have them in our mountain loft to keep us warm when the evenings are cool. I think they smell like a starry evening, one when you want to lie outdoors and look up at the sky."

"Will you take us up with you to the mountains one day, Benito? Florence is exciting but not like climbing to the Casentino and sleeping in the cabin."

"*Certo*. Maybe one day I can come to the city too. Where are these special places where your father liked to read?"

"When he was a little boy and had finished his work, sometimes he would grab his knapsack of books and go to a convent church run by the Dominican monks. The marble windowsills were cool, and from them he could hear the swish swoosh of the friars' long robes. He says reading opens up new worlds to him."

I knew only two worlds, my *Zia* Bianca's cottage and the open air of the summer pastures. As Dante's children talked I turned over every word with wonder. "Tell me about Florence," I said.

"On busy feast days merchants, monks, and landowners gather in the main *piazza*. Crowds of horses, mules, and vendors make their way through the muddy streets, trying to find ways to fit their carts through the twisting narrow alleys. The booksellers' stalls smell the best, like the warm oily sheep aroma Giovanni told us about."

"What do the crowds sound like?" I closed my eyes to imagine myself in Florence. Giovanni was good at imitating. He puffed out his chest and began.

"*Ciao*, there, look out for my cart! *Dio*, how did that pothole trip up my front wheel? Now the woolen cloth I have for sale is as *brutta* and filthy as those pigs running loose. *Attenzione*, up there on the balcony, wait to slosh that laundry pail till I pass this corner." I laughed. Giovanni sounded like a gruff grownup.

Mulling over the strange idea of books as windows to the world, I continued,"Does your papa have favorite books?"

"He carries one little book with him in his knapsack all the time. It's a psalter."

"A what?"

"A psalter, with hymns and psalms from the Bible, all decorated with tiny illustrations in gold, red, and blue. The monks do these decorations in monasteries when they copy books. It takes a long time to make a book and you have to be very skilled to do it. First they copy the writing and then they illuminate the words."

"Why is the psalter his favorite?"

"What makes him happiest are the pages about how we spend our time throughout the year. There is a page for each month. The pictures are small, but they show what kinds of work people do at different times of year. The work is like what we do in the city and up here in the Casentino."

I thought about this. Living and working were things I did, not things I could imagine reading about. My brain skipped around, trying to understand. Further thinking would have to wait, though, because while we were talking Ser Dante returned from visiting his tenants on the farms. He saddled up his horse, thanked *Zia* Bianca, settled Giovanni, Pietro, Iacopo, and Antonia on the two other horses, and they rode off. I had made new friends, and my mind was jumping with new ideas and possibilities.

CHAPTER THREE

UP in the Casentino, Massimo and Antonio and I again delighted in our escape with the sheep and the goats to the high cabin in the summer. Back at *Zia* Bianca's in the fall, we all worked together, children and grownups. We harvested acorns, grapes and olives, and we helped with wine-making and pig-butchering. We chopped wood to prepare for fires in the winter. It wasn't all work. I liked to change chores into games by climbing into trees to shake down ripe nuts, or by holding contests to see who could fill a basket with berries first.

"I can hold a hundred acorns in my tunic!" I shouted as I dropped them one by one inside my shirt collar. "Not even the squirrels are as quick as I am." Antonio told me I looked like a fat *cinghiale* as I walked around with a tunic full of acorns, but I was proud of myself.

In the spring we planted seeds, when the dark earth smelled rich and moist. Late in the day we would lie down in the fields amid the buttercups and daisies that returned every April. We watched cottony clouds float across the sky and pretended they were friendly animals having races. In late summer when baskets overflowed and the sun hung like a ripe peach in the sky, we knew *Zia* Bianca's storehouses would feed us through the winter.

Massimo didn't have to remind me about being a good shepherd to his mama's sheep and goats, and every time I longed to go exploring in the mountains I remembered the snake that had bitten *Papaverito*. Still, though, I was lonely when I went to sleep in my hut behind *Zia* Bianca's house. It wasn't fair that my mama and papa weren't there with me. Especially when I had so much to ask them about what to do, where to go, what to learn, and how to act. Life was a mystery!

The next time Ser Dante came to visit his lands in the Pagnolle, I snatched every chance to talk with his children about life in Florence, and to ask about their father and what he learned from his books.

"Where do you like to go in the city?"

Antonia spoke up first. "My favorite is the Baptistery of San Giovanni, across the street from the cathedral. San Giovanni is the patron saint of Florence, and all babies are baptized there once a year, on his feast day, June twenty-fourth. The walls and ceiling are covered with mosaics, shiny pieces of stone formed into pictures."

"I like *San Miniato al Monte* the best," said Giovanni. "It is a quiet church made of green and white marble high on a hill. From up there the city looks like a puzzle of curving streets, and beyond them the countryside looks like a quilt of olive groves, vineyards, and wheat fields. Red poppies bloom nearby in the summer fields, where birds and bees hum."

"What do you do in the city, after you finish your work?"

Pietro and Iacopo answered together, words tumbling out of their mouths. "We play *carabinieri* with sticks for police clubs, and sometimes we hide upstairs in the loggias and make grunting noises to scare people walking below. When the weather is warm we walk in the hills behind the city and set snares for birds, or we make bows and arrows from tree branches and pretend to be knights in armor." I smiled. This sounded like fun.

"When we fight we take turns being the king of the Guelphs or the king of the Ghibellines," Pietro said.

"Who are they?"

"Civic leaders in Florence. Ask our papa. He knows all about politics. " I had many things to ask Ser Dante about, and resolved to talk with him directly when I had a chance. For the moment, I concentrated on listening to their stories.

"There are bells in the Badia, the abbey near our house, that ring the hours. When we hear them we know it is time to go to church or to school."

"School? I learn what I need to know from *Zia* Bianca and from Massimo. What do you learn at school?"

"I learn Latin, arithmetic, astronomy, music, and writing," Giovanni said. "Since Pietro and Iacopo are younger than I, they haven't started astronomy yet, and since Antonia is a girl, she doesn't go to school at all." I wasn't sure that astronomy and arithmetic would help me much, up in the summer pastures, but maybe music would.

"Why doesn't Antonia go to school?" I asked. In the Casentino girls worked in the fields and climbed trees alongside their brothers. I liked girls, as long as I could run faster than they did, and their having to stay at home didn't seem fair.

"Girls are supposed to learn how to cook and sew and dance, not how to think," said Pietro. I noticed a little curl to his lips and a lift to his eyebrow, and I decided not to ask him about girls any more.

In a few weeks Ser Dante and his children returned to the Casentino. This time I waited to play with them outside until I had had a chance to talk with their papa. "How did you learn to read and write, Ser Dante, and why are words so important to you?"

"Sit down and I will tell you. My parents knew how important language was, so they sent me to school in Florence, just as I now send Giovanni, Pietro, and Iacopo. When I reached my teens I wanted to learn more, so I traveled north over the Apennine Mountains to study at the *Università* in Bologna. I had just settled into my studies there when a messenger arrived from Florence on horseback to bring me the news that my father had suddenly contracted a severe illness and died."

My stomach tightened. "Oh, Ser Dante. I remember how awful I felt when my parents died. My insides were empty, even though *Zia* Bianca welcomed me into her home."

"People are born and people die, Benito. That is part of life. I loved the university, but I needed to return to Florence. As the oldest son I was responsible for my family. Someone had to travel to our lands in Pagnolle, near here, to check on our tenant farmers and collect the rents. My brother Francesco could help some, but he wasn't old enough to do everything."

Maybe Ser Dante was sad sometimes too, like me. I wanted to know more. "What did you want to do, after you had organized your family's business?"

"Near my house in the *sestiere* of San Piero Maggiore is the Via di Calimala housing the foreign cloth guild that provides the rich red robes for the cardinals in the Catholic Church in Rome, the big city to the south of Florence. I dreamed of going to Rome one day to speak for Florentine citizens, although I knew my heart would always be in Florence."

Ser Dante knew what he wanted to do and where he wanted to go. When would I learn what I might try to do? How would I find out? Maybe I wouldn't be good at anything except goatherding. My brain was swimming with new ideas, as if spiders in my head were running in all directions. First ideas of Florence, then Rome. Inside my head the farmlands and hills of the Casentino were shrinking, and around them the rest of Italy was growing and growing, but I felt like a frail minnow in a big wavy lake.

Several weeks later Ser Dante returned to the Casentino on one of his regular visits, and stopped at *Zia* Bianca's door to talk with me. "The Florentines need me to speak for them in Rome," he said. "I serve on the council of priors, and they have asked me to travel to Rome as an emissary to the Pope from the city of Florence. For such an important papal visit I need a trusted servant to accompany me. Benito, you seem eager to help and eager to learn. I want you to go with me to Rome." As he spoke, his arm encircled my shoulder.

My eyes widened and my heart swelled. Rome! In my imagination it was huge and golden. "Ser Dante, do we go today? I will find my shoes. Can I bring the frogs I collected from the brook, the ones that *Zia* Bianca keeps for me in the cracked bowl in the kitchen?" My words were bumpy because I was jumping up and down.

Giovanni shuffled his feet toward the wall, a frown descending on his face. "Papa, why can't *we* go with you? I have been a big help to you here in the Casentino."

"Antonia is only a girl so *she* can't go, but take me!" Pietro said, glaring at his sister, who poked him in the ribs.

"Papa, I am small and I will be no trouble. Can I go?" Iacopo added.

Their father took them aside, sat them down, and spoke to them. "Of course I depend on all of you, both up here on the farms and with your mother at home. That is why I need you to stay here and help. I will count on you to be responsible Alighieri citizens, acting in my place when I am away. Benito has two strong cousins, Massimo and Antonio, to help his *zia*. Besides," he added, "we will bring you some *tortiglioni*, sweet almond cakes, when we return." A flickering smile lit his eyes for just a moment.

Giovanni's shoulders straightened, and Pietro and Iacopo smiled shyly. It was good to know that their father assumed they would act like grownups. They were thinking of the almond cakes too.

"Papa, Benito will be just the boy to go to Rome with you," Giovanni said. "Although he is only nine, like Antonia, he's big for his age and he works hard. Besides, nothing scares him and he always seeks new adventures."

"That's true," Pietro said, "after we hung the barn swing he wanted to build a dam with pebbles in the creek, to see if we could catch tadpoles, and we only stopped and came inside because it started to get dark and we were hungry."

"Have you seen my muscles that make me as strong as an ox?" I asked Ser Dante, flexing my arm into an egg-shaped bump. "I was about to carry the biggest five rocks you have ever seen down to the creek, but Pietro and Iacopo whined like babies and wanted to come inside." Pietro knuckled me in the chest. He didn't want a nine-year-old calling him a baby.

"It was Antonia who got cold and wanted to come in, not me!" Iacopo complained, agreeing with Pietro that I wasn't telling the story exactly as it had happened.

Zia Bianca shook a fist at us. "*Silenzio*," she said. "Dante has an important question for Benito, and he doesn't want to listen to boys who brag and quarrel."

Dante shifted his feet and looked bemused, but said nothing. It was Bianca's job, not his, to discipline children in her own house, whether they belonged to her or not.

"Benito was nice to me, papa," Antonia said. "When the boys called me names, he told them to be nice to girls."

So I was chosen. Turning to me, Ser Dante said we would leave the next morning. Though I could never have imagined the years of challenges ahead, I thought my head would burst from excitement.

CHAPTER FOUR

ALL in the space of a day, Ser Dante arranged with my *zia* for my departure and took me back to Florence with him. I rode behind him in the saddle, with my arms linked tightly around his waist. Giovanni, Pietro, Iacopo, and Antonia were happy to have me visit overnight in their house in Florence, but sad that I was leaving for Rome with their father early the next morning. I think they were still a little envious. Going off to Rome to help their father on a mission to the Pope—THAT was exciting!

Master Dante bought me a mule to ride, and packed warm traveling clothes and food for us both. We named the mule Beffa, or joke, because he had a funny way of looking at us with one ear folded over and one ear straight up. Ser Dante's horse was named Gagliardo, but I called him Galo. At night when I tended the animals in the stable, I whispered in their ears, and Galo was easy to say when making friends with a horse.

"*Olà* Galo, maybe some time when my master is sleeping or off visiting his important people, you and I can go for a gallop. We won't need to tell him." Galo neighed affectionately and stuck out his long tongue to chew the turnip tops I held out for him.

In the saddlebags, Ser Dante added a soft green tunic with lace cuffs for himself for the visit with the Pope. I tucked away the only extra tunic I owned, a plain muslin one that *Zia* Bianca had washed and folded for me. I found room in a corner for a set of dice in case I ever had a spare minute for playing. "Ser Dante," I said, "I will do whatever you ask, and I can groom your horse and my mule every day. I worked in the barn last summer with my cousins, and I know what to do to make animals comfortable. I can clean grit from their horseshoes, feed them, and make their coats smooth and glossy after they sweat." The words burst from my mouth in a torrent. Picturing the adventures ahead made my head swim.

The road south was hilly and rough, but Beffa and I managed to keep up with Ser Dante and Galo. Beffa was sure-footed, and my hands guided him. "You can do it, Beffa! A little leap over this creek, Beffone. I have a carrot and an apple in my bag to share with you after we make it up this hill." My feet barely hung below Beffa's belly, so I urged him on with my knees. I was tired by nightfall and my legs ached, but I didn't complain.

When Ser Dante and I settled for the night, I grabbed the chance to ask him more questions. "Ser Dante," I said, "I hear you know a lot about something Giovanni called 'politics,' but I don't know what that is. Can you tell me?"

"Politics means governing well in my home city of Florence. I am proud of our city and I want it to be strong and independent. Sometimes that means we Florentines have to defend our government in battle."

"With swords and blood?" I asked.

"Sometimes, yes. Other times we fight with words to persuade citizens to make good laws to govern themselves."

"Tell me about the sword fights first," I said as I curled my knees up against my chest. The night was dark and chilly.

"When I was young I fought in one of the bloodiest battles ever. It happened in a place called Campaldino, not far from your *Zia* Bianca's house. The Aretines—people from Arezzo—were trying to take over Florence, so I marshaled the Florentine Guelphs to fight the Aretine Ghibellines."

So this is where Pietro and Giovanni and Iacopo found out about Guelphs and Ghibellines, when they played make-believe war with their sticks. I thought about the sunny fields and pastures in the Casentino and tried to imagine them filled with racing horses and shouting soldiers. My eyes narrowed and my stomach cramped. In wars people were killed, but if Ser Dante was fighting for the honor of Florence, maybe something good could be the result. Still, I didn't like thinking of the wheat fields thick with blood.

"Who are the Guelphs and the Ghibellines, Ser Dante?"

"The white Guelphs stand for moderation and patriotism. That means they don't want to do really bad things, and that they want to keep Florence safe. I believe in them, and that's why I was chosen to be one of the six 'priors' responsible for city government in Florence."

I wondered why, if the Guelphs wanted to do good things, they fought in wars, but it didn't seem right to ask. "What does a 'prior' do?"

"We make decisions about what is best for the city's defenses, like building walls, equipping guards, and making money." Ser Dante's words circled in my brain, but I couldn't find a clear path for them through my fuzzy thoughts. I snuggled up against Beffa's belly and went to sleep.

The next morning we packed up our belongings in the saddlebags and continued south to Rome. The mountain path we followed leveled out in mid-morning into a broad meadow, so I rode along lazily next to Ser Dante.

"Why doesn't Antonia go to school along with Giovanni and Pietro and Iacopo?"

"In Florence, most people think that girls should stay home and learn sewing and dancing and cooking, but I don't agree with them, so I myself am teaching Antonia how to read." Ser Dante was quiet for a moment. Then he spoke up again. "Let me tell you about a special girl I knew when I was a boy like you," he said. "I thought girls were mysterious but fascinating too."

I looked over at Ser Dante over Beffa's pointed ears. "Who was she?"

"Her name was Beatrice Portinari, and her family owned a *palazzo*, grander than our house. I met her when we were both only nine years old, about the same age as you. She went every day to the church of Santa Margherita, beyond the neighborhood church of San Martino where my family worshipped. I used to plead with my father to go to Santa Margherita just so I could sit next to Beatrice, hoping she would talk to me." I giggled. Girls were fine, but it seemed silly to be attracted to one in particular. Still, I wanted to hear the rest of the story.

"What happened?"

"On May Day in the year 1274 Beatrice's father hosted a party for the whole *sestiere* to welcome spring's return, and my father and I went. I took my knapsack, the one I always carried with me holding my pens and scraps of paper so I could write down things I wanted to remember."

Ser Dante eyes wandered off and he seemed to be dreaming more than speaking to me, but I kept asking questions. "Did Beatrice talk to you?"

"No, she didn't, but my face turned red and my hands were sweating when I saw her. I couldn't decide if she was a girl or an angel." I giggled again, but quietly. Whoever saw an angel? Were there really such things? Ser Dante continued. "I still have the wrinkled paper on which I wrote about her that day. Her hair was like gold and her arms were pure white. She wore flowers and a beautiful dress with a red belt, and the glow surrounding her made her seem to be the daughter of a god. Do you realize, Benito, that her name in our musical Tuscan language, *beata*, means the blessed one?"

"*Zia* Bianca says my name has to do with blessings too. Beyond her cottage loom the *Alpe di San Benedetto*, the high mountains of the blessed saint after whom I am named."

Although Ser Dante seemed to speak to the trees and the birds rather than to me, he must have wanted me to hear his words, because he continued talking. "To me Beatrice seemed to float when she walked, so that her feet barely touched the cobblestones." I didn't dare giggle any more, but I kept asking him questions about his angelic girl.

"Does she still live in Florence near you?"

"No, she married someone else and then she died young. Everyone thought I would outgrow my love for her, but I still write about her in my poetry."

Here was a new word for me to ask about. "What is poetry?"

"My poetry tells stories and ideas." I waited a moment, and then I asked Ser Dante if he would read some of his poetry to me.

"Above Florence is a place that Giovanni and I like to visit…the church of San Miniato, surrounded by flowers in the spring and summer. I watched the poppies open and close on their stems, as the sun first touched them in the morning, and I wrote about them:

As little flowers, bent down and closed by the frost of night,
stand up, all open on their stems,
when the sun comes back to warm and brighten them."

I tasted the words on my tongue, trying to imagine the flowers opening and closing. How amazing that a poet could capture nature with words! Maybe his pen had a magical power. What else might words be able to accomplish? I wanted to learn more about words and more about Ser Dante.

CHAPTER FIVE

THE next day the sun beat down on us so fiercely at midday that Ser Dante said we should rest until late afternoon before continuing. He chose a spot close to a stream, shaded by willows.

As I lay on the creek bank I turned my head toward him and asked again about Beatrice and about his poetry. "Isn't it sad, writing about Beatrice when she isn't around any more? Did you ever see her again after that first time, at the party in her father's *palazzo*?"

He answered slowly. "I did see her once, dressed in white, walking in the street with two other ladies. She nodded to me courteously, so I think she remembered me from our childhood. However, soon her family arranged her marriage to someone else. All I can do is glorify her in my poetry. Here, I will read some.

Love is encompassed in my Lady's eyes
Whence she ennobles all she looks upon.
Where e'er she walks, the gaze of everyone she draws"

I tried not to notice the mistiness in his eyes. "I know nothing of marriage, but why didn't you marry her?" I asked.

"Marriages are arranged by families to form useful and prosperous alliances. Loving one another may be an ideal, but marriage is a contract. Anyway, I couldn't have married Beatrice. Years before, in 1277 when I was only eleven, my father had betrothed me to Gemma Donati, now my wife and the mother of your friends. Gemma was only ten then, so the marriage was postponed until we were both older. Our parents were pleased with the match because the Donati family lived near us and owned lands in Pagnolle near ours."

I didn't want to intrude on Ser Dante's closest feelings, but I had to know. "Wasn't it hard to forget about Beatrice?"

"I never forget her. Instead, I write poetry. There, I can make Beatrice into a symbol of divine perfection." I wondered what a symbol was, but I didn't ask. Ser Dante continued. " Gemma has been a good wife to me and a good mother for our children. I think of Beatrice only with my words." Although this made sense, I still felt sad. I remembered what Ser Dante had said about imagining Beatrice floating over the cobblestone streets, and about how she was more like an angel than a woman. I decided to ask him about Gemma instead.

"What will you bring home for Gemma from our trip to Rome?" I knew that Giovanni, Pietro, Iacopo, and Antonia were looking forward to their almond cakes, but what would a wife want? Maybe having her husband return home safe would be enough.

"I brought her gifts from the Casentino already…a baby lamb, and a basket of apples. She works hard to keep our family fed and clothed, but she doesn't understand much about politics or writing. I try to provide for my family as best I can." His voice began to sound distant, and I guessed that he did not write about Gemma in his poetry.

Getting to know Ser Dante was like peeling an onion and finding more and more layers. I wanted to peer inside him to know more. He loved his family, his writing, his farms, and his city of Florence. I cared about my adopted family too, at *Zia* Bianca's house, but her plots of farmland and my cousins began to seem far away. New thoughts crowded into my brain. Ser Dante's words opened two new worlds for me—one, the road to Rome on which we were traveling, and the other a world inside myself. I hoped he would grow to love me too, but I would have to prove worthy. *Papaverito* loved me, but he was just a goat so his love was simple, not complicated like Ser Dante's loves.

By the next evening we had arrived in Rome, where I made friends with the scullery boys in the inn. Beffa leaned his velvety nose over my shoulder, and the Roman boys laughed at his funny ears. "Your donkey, your *asinello*, must have gotten his head stuck in the olive press." They pronounced the "s" in *asinello* sharply, not like the soft "z" sound I was used to hearing up north in Tuscany.

"He is the best mule in the world," I told them, "and he can outrun any of your Roman donkeys. Galo can too."

"Let's see how fast Galo can run," the biggest boy said as he leaned toward me with a menacing look. "My stallion can beat him any day. How about a midnight race? I'll bet you your extra tunic against my leather jerkin."

I was afraid and brave at the same time. Though I was supposed to be resting Galo for the ride back north, I couldn't resist the chance to race. "*Bene*, I'll get his bridle. Where shall we meet?"

"Near the *Colosseo*, in four hours. Two times around and I'll be off with your tunic, *ragazzino*."

I didn't like the round-faced Roman's term "little boy," and I couldn't resist yelling back at him, "You'll be sorry, you *zuccone* you!" The word—pumpkin head—wasn't mean, but it did make him sound like a big oaf. He flushed a deep red and jammed his hands together as he stalked off.

Now I had to take Galo to the race, though Master Dante had forbidden me to take Beffa or Galo out at night. I worried as I led Galo out quietly, not waking the stableboys. At the *Colosseo* the only sounds were the hooting of owls and the meowing of cats. Why had I agreed to this challenge? Master Dante would be angry. It was too late though. I had to go through with it.

Galo stepped proudly up to the start and I spurred him on, around the outside walls of the big arena two times. The Roman boy was heavy. His horse labored beneath him while I flew on, light as a feather on Galo's broad back.

"I win the jerkin!" I said as Galo pulled up slightly ahead, sweating and heaving.

The next morning I slept late, and scurried to get Beffa and Galo ready for the ride north. Master Dante saw the leather jerkin and noticed dust on Gagliardo's flanks. "Where have you been, Benito? Weren't you sleeping here in the stable all night?"

I hung my head and stammered in explanation. "I…I didn't want to be called a little boy. But master, it was so thrilling riding Galo so fast in the middle of the night!"

"Take it back at once, and apologize, Benito. If you are to come with me as a helper, you must do as I say. Gagliardo should have been ready for a rough ride after I see the Pope tomorrow, and you should have been resting too."

I found the round-headed Roman boy asleep and poked him gently. "I shouldn't have called you a *zuccone*," I said. "Here is your jerkin; it is too fine for me. I am sorry."

The next day I followed my master to his meeting with the Pope, leading Beffa and Galo to the gates of the Lateran Palace. I was glad when Ser Dante went in, because I could talk with Beffa and with Galo in their stroking and whinnying language. Ser Dante did not want to talk with me that morning.

When he came out his eyes looked straight ahead and his jaw was set as we turned to begin our travels back toward Tuscany. My heart sank. Maybe he thought he had made a mistake to bring along a young boy like me. I wanted to please Ser Dante, and visiting Rome had set my body and my brain on fire. *Zia* Bianca's chicken soup was the best, but I didn't want to go back.

What if I had ruined my chances to go adventuring? How could I explain to Giovanni and Pietro and Iacopo and Antonia that I could not live up to what their father hoped of me? The world was closing in, making my eyes grow big and round.

When we stopped at midday for a rest, Ser Dante still had not uttered a word, but the silence had been screaming at me. At last he turned, and with sadness in his voice asked, "If you wish, Benito, I can take you back to the Casentino where life is easier and where you have playmates. Perhaps you wouldn't have been tempted to race Gagliardo if those big Roman boys hadn't teased you."

My eyes welled with tears as I hurried to answer. "Oh, Ser Dante, please do not send me back. I want so much to travel and to help you, and I promise to listen and learn."

I tied Beffa and Galo's ropes to a tree and lifted the saddlebags down. My master had closed his eyes, and I seized a chance to prove myself. After I fed and watered the animals, I ran through the underbrush to a nearby brook, where I made a net of twigs. Soon a glistening pink *trota*, that kind of trout common to Tuscan streams, swam by, fintailing gently in the dappled light. I thrust in my net and caught him on the second try. By the time I hurried back to Ser Dante with my prize, he was waking up from his nap. "What have you here? You should have been resting too, but what a meal you have snagged for us!"

My face turned the color of the *trota*, but I remembered a favorite proverb of my father's. "*Chi dorme non piglia pesci,*" I said with a little smile, "He who sleeps catches no fish." Ser Dante's mouth curved into a smile too, as he realized how much I was trying to please him. "Master, you can count on me. I vow to stay with you and do your bidding always. You have my solemn promise." I folded my arm across my heart as I spoke.

"We understand each other and from now on you will do as I ask. We will be a strong team," my master said as he started the fire to cook the *trota*.

I gasped with relief, saying, "I will cook the fish, master, but after we eat may I have a nap, to catch up with you? My eyelids feel like rocks." I hoped that Ser Dante and I had become friends.

CHAPTER SIX

BURSTING with chances to show my worthiness, I threw my soul into serving Ser Dante. The Pope had ordered us to visit San Gimignano, on our way back to Florence. "Whatever you wish I will do for you….and more if I can," I said. Ser Dante only smiled, but I thought I glimpsed a sparkle in his eye.

When I looked up from a distance at the hilltop town, the *città delle belle torri*, bristling with tall towers, I thought it looked like the head of a giant porcupine, cresting the hill with spiky armor. "Ser Dante, will this fierce city let us in?"

"We have a job to do here and the *cittadini,* citizens, should welcome us. I'll tell you why they must listen to me."

"Why are there so many towers?"

"A powerful family lives in each one, and members of the family can retreat into their tower if they are attacked. Much of the city's life takes place inside the towers instead of on the streets as it does in Florence."

"But how could I move from one tower to another to visit my friends?"

"There are some toeholds in most of the towers to hold wooden catwalks, if one is brave enough to balance himself high above the streets."

"Since I can walk across a stream on slippery rocks, I could do that!"

"The people of San Gimignano also use those toeholds to attach drying lines for their famous textiles, dyed yellow with *zafferano*, saffron. In my view, the way houses are arranged in Florence is better. To have a stable town government people should cooperate with one another instead of maintaining individual fortresses. In Florence we have a more democratic way of life than that here in San Gimignano."

I imagined myself walking on tightropes between towers, making my way between billowing sheets of gold cloth. "Life in San Gimignano could be fun," I said.

My master had more serious work to do. His task was to persuade the leaders of San Gimignano to join the white Guelph party. After we finished the steep climb up to the town, I watched in awe as he stood on the city ramparts, exhorting everyone there to join forces with the Florentines. "Alone, none of us can achieve the ideals of fair and good government for which we all strive," he said, "but together we can build a greater community answering to everyone's needs. We will be like the individual stones making up a strong fortress wall."

After his speech, Master Dante left the animals in my care. I fed and groomed them, and collected walnuts and raspberries for our trip the next day. While I made these preparations, Ser Dante walked through the streets beneath the towers, calling again for the people of San Gimignano to join with the Florentines. He believed in his ideals and he spoke with passion. Watching from a distance, I saw how his eyes gleamed and his voice deepened. "Join with us, my fellow Tuscans! Together we can keep out the German emperors and the Ghibelline forces helping them, but alone we may perish." His words reminded me of the mountain pastures in the Casentino, where if the flocks stayed together, wolves would find it harder to attack. The words made sense.

After giving his speech Ser Dante gathered me, Beffa, and Gagliardo, and headed for a campground outside the town walls. "I will write a few lines," he said, pulling out his quills and paper. "Writing poetry carves out a safe place for me, and San Gimignano especially stirs me to write, since it is the home of my favorite poet, Folgore." Pulling out a small book from his pack, he read aloud some of Folgore's poems. My ears prickled, because many of them were about children's games, like the ones I played in the Casentino with my cousins. The verses I liked best told how boys in San Gimignano hunted and fished in the summer, and how they threw snowballs in the winter. Children must be the same everywhere, exploring the same cycles of fun throughout the year.

"Ser Dante, I like the idea that poems are about fun as well as about hopes or problems," I said, "and hearing them makes me feel as if I have friends all over these mountains."

He must have been feeling satisfied. "Benito, you are well named, as your name comes from *benedire*, to bless. You have truly become a blessing to me on this trip."

"Benito is my *soprannome*, my nickname," I said. "I don't know about blessing, but I do know that with you I have gone to new places and made new friends. You have become a special friend, Ser Dante, if I may say so."

"Look here, Benito," said my master, holding out the writing quill, "I will teach you to read and write. This is the letter 'B' for your name. You will need to read and write to help me deliver messages, and one day you may learn to read poetry and grow to love it as I do."

Back in Florence, the black Guelphs grew stronger and more antagonistic, threatening the peaceful regime my master envisioned. Again he traveled to Rome as ambassador to the Pope, this time with me as a seasoned servant who, though small, knew how to read and write—at least basic words.

"To return to Rome is an honor I cannot turn down," Master Dante said to his wife Gemma as he packed for his second trip south, "and all the Florentines will benefit from this important work. Benito will help me, and I know you will care for our home and the children while I am away."

Giovanni, Pietro, Iacopo, and Antonia joined me outside the door, to ask about my travels with their father and Beffa and Galo. "Has he been good to you?" "Have you ever been attacked by pirates on the road?" "How can you get Beffa to climb up a mountainside?" "Have you met any other children?" "How did you celebrate your tenth birthday last March?"

I answered their questions as best I could. I did miss them, and traveling with their father was hard work. But I liked it. I listened respectfully at the door while he talked with Gemma, and then I ran back to the stable to ready Galo and Beffa for another journey south. Maybe we will meet bandits this time, I thought, and perhaps my master and I will have to jump in Lake Trasimeno and have to swim to escape. The idea was exhilarating, and I hoped it would happen.

But this time terror struck. While we were gone, the black Guelphs usurped power in the city of Florence, burning homes, assassinating enemies, and destroying property. Master Dante's enemies invented charges against him, claiming among other things that he was guilty of barratry, or accepting bribes for political promotion. On our way back to Florence in 1302 after his diplomatic duties in Rome, he and I heard the awful news while traveling through Siena.

A messenger on horseback raced into the shell-shaped central *piazza*, his mount's flanks heaving as the reins pulled him to a clattering stop outside the inn where Ser Dante and I were staying. "Dante," the horseman panted, "chaos reigns in Florence! The enemies have seized the homes and places of business of the white Guelph leaders. Do not worry; Gemma and the children are safe. Your brother Francesco helped them escape to the Casentino to your lands there for temporary shelter. But much of the city is in flames, and some Guelphs have been hanged and others mutilated. You must never set foot inside the city of Florence again."

Ser Dante's eyes narrowed and his face turned pale as he digested these words. "Surely," he said to the horseman, "these enemies can be defeated and we will regain control in the city."

"No, *signore*, it is not possible. The Ghibellines rage like animals throughout the city, and they pin their grievances on you as leader. They have issued a decree of banishment."

"Those mean black Guelphs!" I cried as I clung to Beffa for warmth and support and huddled close to Master Dante. "What is 'banishment,' master?"

"Hush," Dante said, riveting his attention on the messenger. "Banishment?"

he repeated.

"I have not told you all," the horseman replied. "The decree against you is not only banishment, but banishment with condemnation to death if you ever enter Florentine territory again."

"Death?" Dante said.

Tears formed in my eyes, but I choked them back, wanting to appear brave.

"Yes. The Ghibelline leaders have declared that you are an enemy of the state and that if you ever set foot in your native city again, you will be killed on the spot, in as painful and lingering a way as possible," the messenger said.

The verdict began to sink into Ser Dante's heart and soul. I would only later begin to realize that the horseman's words meant the biggest change my master and I had ever experienced. This banishment, exile, *esilio,* would be a catastrophe for his work, his family, and his life. Could this really be happening to him? I had felt like that when I learned that my father and mother had died. Gradually it became clear to him that the news was true: he was exiled. He was never to enter his beloved city of Florence again, and I must go with him. I had just begun to savor my new life of adventure with Ser Dante, but now the walls were closing in on us and fear took over. Nonetheless, I had promised to stay with him and I vowed to keep my promise.

That night my legs ached from the ride north, and my head ached too. I drank some warm *minestrone*, vegetable soup, and lay down on a straw pallet by my master's bed in our small room at the inn. Thoughts of wandering in exile ran through my head, mixed with visions of dragons and knights and battles, but soon fatigue won out. Master Dante covered me with the warm sheepskin he carried in his saddlebag, and I fell into a deep sleep.

He told me the next morning that sleep had never come for him that night. Since he could not sleep, he lit a candle in the room, pulled a quill from his pack, and sketched some lines for later use in his poem:

so you will have to leave Florence.
You will leave everything loved most dearly;
and this is the arrow
that the bow of exile shoots first.

I suspect that only his reflective nature and his sense of stability kept him from tears as the agonizing reality of banishment took over in his mind. I cried when he read the lines to me. His entire ordered world had been contained within Florence's walls, and that world now dissolved.

The next morning I saw only a stub where the candle had been. Ser Dante told me that the candlelight flickered and went out near dawn, as the harshness of the decree became real in his mind. It would become clear to me later, as we traveled from place to place, how much he longed for the warmth and familiarity of Florentine cooking and Florentine wine, busy Florentine streets, Florentine holidays, and—most of all—Florentine civic pride. He could never return to his own city or to his family and allies again. I too was away from my home and my *Zia* Bianca and my cousins, but I had chosen to go with him, to have new adventures. Ser Dante's situation was different. He longed to go home. Sentenced to exile, what was he to do? By morning his anger at those who had tricked and abandoned him settled into loneliness. I smiled when he told me that he felt consoled when he remembered that at least he had me, his faithful servant Benito, and that he had leaned over to touch my shoulder during the night as I slept.

He told me that thoughts had raced in his head throughout the night. How will Benito and I survive, where will we go, what will we eat, who will befriend us, how can we help revivify the civic glory that is Florence? "Benito," he said, "as the sun came up I decided what I can do: write." He told me that he would write about his woes, his thoughts, his hopes, and his travels. He would continue to teach me more about reading and writing as he threw himself into writing his long poem.

"Writing is powerful," he said. "Through the power of words the enemies of Florence can be defeated, the champions of Florence can be exalted, and the civic grandeur of the city can be revitalized. My poem will take on grander tasks as well, justifying the evils done to innocent victims, explaining the relationship between God and the state, and charting a course for personal salvation."

It sounded like an impossibly big task to me, and I didn't understand everything. Still, I could tell that his plan comforted him.

"Good for you, Master," I said. The things he was telling me hovered around him like a warm blanket.

"Perhaps as we travel the hills and valleys around Florence, Benito, we can become part of the rhythms and cycles of work described in Folgore's poems and in my psalter."

"Ser Dante, I believe you and I hope what you say is true. I will try to make your life easier however I can," I said. Tears came to my eyes. I wasn't sure a young boy like me could do much, but I was determined to help.

The next day Master Dante told me that one of the things he most hoped for was that his reputation would be made good again to his family in Florence. Stopping outside Siena in the morning, he drew me close beneath his shoulder and wrote a fervent plea in his poetry notes:

And I ask by what you long for most,
if ever you tread the land of Tuscany,
that you restore my good name to my kindred.

With a heavy heart my master began his travels with me, noting in his poetry papers, *"In truth I set out without a sail and without a rudder, carried to faraway ports and shores by the dry wind breathed by sad poverty."*

CHAPTER SEVEN

"MASTER, how do you know where we are going?" I asked as we led Beffa and Gagliardo up a rocky path north of Siena. My bare legs shivered a little in the cold, and my teeth chattered. Dante had given me an extra saddle blanket to cover my shoulders, but the wind nipped in around my knees and wrists. Doubt made my heart chilly too. Where would we sleep, and what would we eat? I had vowed loyalty to my master, but the mountains were dark and scary. To fortify my resolve I remembered my talks with Giovanni and Pietro and Iacopo and Antonia about the adventures I'd had with their father on our trip to Rome. The swirling ideas in my head made me giddy, and my stomach was growling too. Then I imagined my *Zia* Bianca's *spaghetti alla carbonara*, full of savory bacon. This was both good and bad. My mouth dripped, wanting to taste it, but creating it in my mind satisfied my hunger a little. Maybe this kind of imaginary creating was like what my master did with his poems, when he took out his quills to write. I began to feel better.

Answering my question, Ser Dante said, "We must trust in Beffa and Gagliardo to find a good way, and we must trust each other. We are not facing the mountains alone." That night as we rolled out our blankets in a cave and warmed some dried beef over a fire, Ser Dante took out his quill and wrote:

We went over the solitary plain
like men returning to the road they have lost
who, until they get there, seem to walk in vain.

It was winter when we set out, toward Verona far to the north beyond the Apennine Mountains, Dante said. First we wandered into the foothills west of the Casentino and then into thick woods and rocky terrain. Sometimes I jumped off Beffa's bony back and led him over stony rises, but more often he felt his own way with careful hoofprints. My master said that beyond the mountains lay the broad agricultural plain formed by the sweep of the Po River toward the Adriatic. In Verona, a city along the Adige River in the northern part of that plain, lived political allies of the white Guelph party. He and I could take refuge there. I believed him but my heart still fluttered.

"Master, what do you think *Zia* Bianca is doing right now?" I said, edging Beffa along a rocky ledge. "I wonder if Massimo and Antonio know what has happened to us?"

"I am sure that fellow Florentines will tell them we have been exiled. We are safe in the mountains."

I looked down at my feet and wiggled my toes to keep them warm. Up in the Casentino with my aunt and my cousins my days had been simpler. Maybe I had been wrong to jump at the chance to go with Ser Dante as a helper. I gritted my teeth but didn't say anything. I had promised to serve him loyally, and I intended to keep my promise.

My master hoped we would find a welcome somewhere during our journey north, perhaps in one of the mountain monasteries like the one at Camaldoli. He said that holy men lived there, dedicating their lives to poverty, prayer, and learning. Even if they knew of the political plot against Ser Dante, compassion would not allow them to take sides in a partisan fight. Their way of life was remote from the bustling activity in the urban centers below. If my master could find such a place, the monks might take us in. But, I thought, monks probably don't like to climb trees or swing on ropes.

"Keep your eyes open for signs of a monastery," Ser Dante said. On our way north we may want to stay with the monks. We can do some work for them in exchange for replenishing our supplies."

"*Zia* Bianca taught me how to mend cooking pots and wine casks, and how to hang ham, *prosciutto,* for aging. And will the monks have horses? Then Beffa and Galo will have company too, and I can help with grooming in the stables." The thought cheered me.

"You will be a great help to any mountain dwellers we may find," Ser Dante replied. "I, too, have some skills the monks may need. The monasteries are centers for the preservation of books, and I know how to repair soiled and torn manuscript pages." Although his words ended, his thought continued. Perhaps the peace of communing with the monks, high up in isolation in the mountains where few visitors ever came, would soothe the heartaches of our exile.

"Benito, we will take our chances. If we don't find a monastery, perhaps we can find shelter with a lord in a castle hidden in these mountains. Our fate is in our own hands, but we can also take advantage of any opportunities that arise."

Ser Dante knew of a grand fortified castle at Poppi, and of others nearby at Romena and Porciano. Without a map and in the mountain winter it would be hard to locate either a monastery or a castle; but if luck were with us, we could find such a place, rest, eat and sleep. And we would be warm, I thought as I rubbed my hands together against the cold. Patting Beffa's flank helped too.

I was determined to stay with my master, but that didn't stop my mind and my stomach from growling. I still had doubts. "Master, what will happen to us if we don't find any mountain men?" I asked. Not wanting Ser Dante to worry, I tried to sound hopeful. "I can try to set some rabbit traps for food for us, and there must be clear water in the streams."

"If we locate neither a monastery nor a castle, we will move on over the mountains and down into the Po valley until we find a welcome community. In the inside pocket of my saddlebag there are some extra *biscotti*. We will not starve." Ser Dante figured that if we kept the sunrise to our right, we would be moving in a northerly direction.

Where possible, I rode along right behind my master, or sometimes ahead of him if Beffa could find his footing better than Gagliardo. Where steep inclines and rocky outcroppings made riding impossible, we both dismounted and walked. Beffa took the lead then, finding the best footholds for all four of us. I patted his prickly flank. What a good donkey he was! Sometimes I hugged him too, because his soft nose was warm and comforting.

"Master, will we be even colder as we climb higher?" I asked as the wind howled around our ears and chilled my ankles and wrists. Ser Dante took off his own outer woolen tunic and draped it over my shoulders.

"Soon we will find a camping place where we can build a fire and warm ourselves," he replied. I thought wistfully of the thick leather jerkin I had returned to the boy in Rome who had challenged me and Galo. I should not have taken Galo out for the midnight race, and my master had been right to tell me to return the jerkin, but nonetheless how warm it would have kept me up here in the mountains!

By late afternoon we came across an overhang that would shelter us for the night. Drifts of frozen leaves provided some bedding, and we foraged for nuts and berries under the snow, in addition to grass for Beffa and Gagliardo. I kept my fingers and toes as close to the small fire as I could.

In the morning we moved on, away from Florence, climbing higher and higher in the mountains. Three days passed, but we came across neither a monastery nor a castle. We had eaten all the biscotti by the second day, and I began talking to my stomach. "Hush, now! Food will be coming!" I was accustomed to listening for birds, rabbits, and snakes in the hills of the Casentino, but here even my keen ear detected no unusual sound. Quiet reigned in these mountains. All we heard was the crisp crunching of the animals' hooves in the snow, and all we saw through the frosty steam of our own breath was the rugged path in front of us.

Fortunately, the next evening we reached a weathered empty shed. Ser Dante said it must have been used by goatherds who came up into these mountains with their flocks for summer grazing. "This can be our castle, Master," I said. Beneath my pinched smile, though, I was cold and tired. Ser Dante lost heart too. Perhaps we would be hermits forever. As I fell asleep I heard the hooting of owls in the trees outside, or was it something else? A strange cry whistled through the cracks in the walls of the shed, but I was too tired to worry.

I awoke with a start to see a huge ragged man standing over me, shouting, "What are you doing in my barn? This is my property, get out at once!" His clothes were dirty and he smelled of too much wine.

I rolled over next to my master, who stood up facing the man and said, "*Scusi*, signore. We mean no harm. We are only tired travelers."

"*Ahi*, no. You must be some of those double-crossing spies sent from the King of Naples. I have orders to look out for you and to kill any couriers coming this way over the mountains." He pulled out a long knife and sharpened it on a heavy pipe hanging on a leather thong from his belt. I thought my eyes would burst out of my head.

Ser Dante pulled me behind him and stretched out his arms to show the man we had no weapons. "*Compassione, signore,* we are godly people and we seek only peace."

"Nonsense!" said the man, who towered over me like a shaggy giant. "What good would God do you anyway? My blows will send you to hell where you belong, and your god won't help you."

I knew my master was a good fighter, but it was clear that we couldn't escape by fighting. "*Signore*," I said, using the polite title that the rough man didn't deserve, "if we *were* spies we would be traveling at night and sleeping in the day. And I have no pockets to carry any spying letters, look!" I pulled up my tunic to show I had barely enough clothing to cover my thin body.

"But you, *sporcaccione*, dirty pig," he said to Ser Dante, "what have YOU?"

My master pulled out his papers. "They are only poems. See, there is no seal from the king of Naples or from any other official."

Owls hooted outside, along with the howling of a wolf or mountain lion. "Go, then," screamed the man, "take your lies and go out to face the wolves." Ser Dante and

I seized our chance and moved to the door with our belongings as fast as we could. We untied Beffa and Gagliardo and flew into the darkness.

All the time we were running I thought I could see the scowling face of the huge man right beside me, and each gust of wind seemed like a slash from his knife. Ser Dante told me the noises we heard were just the night owls, but I thought they were cries from creatures tormented in the dark. Terror made my feet nimble, though, and we made good time. By daybreak we stopped, exhausted but safe.

"He was a bad man, and we are fortunate to have escaped," Ser Dante said.

"Master, why are there such bad people?" I asked. His face clouded and he told me that he had not believed it himself until he had heard of the burning and killing in Florence.

"Most people are good at heart," he said, "but you must always be alert, because there is much evil in the world."

On the fourth day, cutting through the ice in a stream, my master lowered his water flask for refilling. As he looked at the swift current beneath the frozen crust, he noticed in surprise that it was running north, away from Florence, not back to the south, the direction from which we had come. "Benito, come quickly and look! We must have hiked over the crest and are now descending into the valley."

"Bravo, *padrone*!" I replied. "Beffa and Galo will go faster downhill, and you and I will feel lighter than sparrows. Already I am not so hungry, and my toes are warmer with every step."

"We will walk beyond the Po and over the frozen wheat fields to the city of Verona," he told me. Florentine friends had told him that benevolent lords ruled there—the Princes of the Scala. "We will look for the sign of the Scaligeri family, the eagle over the *scala* or ladder, and visit their prince. Verona will not be Florence, but perhaps the Veronese people can help us."

I pictured returning to city life and sleeping on a straw pallet. "Master, we will even eat baked bread once again!" I cried with delight.

"This is true, my son, but you must be aware that the bread of the north is not the same as the bread in Tuscany, where we do not add salt to the yeast dough."

As we gave water to Gagliardo and Beffa to ready them for the climb down the mountain, Ser Dante scribbled some notes to use in his poems:

You will learn how salty the bread tastes
in others' houses, and how hard
is the going up and down of others' stairs.

The north-facing slopes gradually leveled out, giving way to open plains stretching toward the river valley. I spotted some fields and even some peach orchards. When we stopped to refill our water flasks at a well, we met two youths who offered us food and spoke to us warmly, in the sharper Italian dialect of the north. "Here, *signore*, here, *fratellino*, little brother, taste some of our lunch."

"Master, how yummy these dried peaches are!" I exclaimed as my teeth crunched as fast as they could, to make room in my mouth for some of the bread.

"Do not forget your manners. Before we eat, we owe our friends great thanks, *ringraziamenti*, for sharing their meal with us." I reddened and lowered my eyes, but extended my small hand to the strangers in thanks.

"*Mi dispiace*, I am sorry, *signori*. We have been in the mountains a long time and I forgot how to act."

CHAPTER EIGHT

IN the distance Ser Dante and I could see the city of Verona, with sunlight reflecting on its warm yellow-brown walls. Reaching the city, we headed straight toward the busy market center, where women and children bought and sold fresh vegetables.

"*Mangia qui*! Eat here! We sell the best meat! Buy from us!" the vendors shouted in the *Piazza delle Erbe*, the plaza of herbs and vegetables. We two travelers thrust ourselves into the welcome flurry of the marketplace. My master accepted some refreshing gulps of the local Soave, a white wine, and Valpolicella, a red one.

"Here, *figliuolo*, you need to taste this too. Just a few swallows."

Catching a glimpse of a red marble *campanile* or tower visible to the northwest, Ser Dante made his way toward it. We made a bedraggled, tired, and dirty foursome—a young boy, a wiry and muscular poet, and two weary animals—but our eyes shone with excitement. On our way west from the marketplace we passed a large Roman amphitheater and peered inside to see the vast arena and tiers of stone benches. "My son, a grand government flourished here long before our time, but some of this arena has long since crumbled into dust."

"It is like the *Colosseo* in Rome, Master," I replied, remembering with embarrassment my night ride there. "Why don't the people rebuild it? It would be a grand place to have festivals and parades."

"One government falls and another one rises. The world always changes, whether for better or for worse." The thought may have occurred to him that civilization was fragile, like life, but he didn't say so.

Continuing toward the *campanile* and its adjacent tower, we reached a quiet and pleasant square near the river, facing a monumental church near the banks of the still mostly frozen Adige River. San Zeno, my master read at the entrance. Its imposing but plain façade featured an entrance porch framed with carved stone panels, below an elaborate rose window. Ser Dante peered closely at the scenes on both sides of the arched doorway. Later he told me he had been wondering why they didn't illustrate biblical stories like most church decorations. What did the carvings depict, and what would churchgoers learn from them?

"What are you doing, master?" I asked. I was more interested in the stray kittens playing on the piazza than I was in carvings. Besides, a group of boys kicked a ball around in the distance, gradually coming near the church entrance.

A young Veronese boy, perhaps around twelve, saw my master looking at the carvings and stepped away from his group of playing friends. "*Scusi, signore,*" he said politely to Ser Dante, "where have you come from and why do the carvings on this church entrance interest you so much?"

I left the kittens and moved closer to listen. "Art always appeals to me," Ser Dante said. "What can you tell me about the sculpture, son?"

"Well," the lad said, "there are twelve squares here, six on the left and six on the right, high up above the archways. Each panel shows a man working during a particular month. The figures are stubby and fat and more like dolls than people, and the plants and animals are flat. Still, they show how my cousins and friends in the country live and work. Inside the church most of the decorations are about the Bible, but out here they are about real life. Sometimes my friends and I play games in this piazza, acting out scenes from the carvings for each other to guess. The hardest to do is October, with the two hogs, because someone has to act like a pig. My little brother likes that part the best." I smiled and moved in to listen more closely.

"After we play around the carvings, I like to go out in the country to see how the pictures carved here are like the work that my family does in the *campagna* around Verona."

Ser Dante smiled. This boy shared his own fascination with the cycles of work and of nature. The boy and the man moved slowly from panel to panel, admiring the detailed representations. Each scene was framed by a carved arch and columns, and was labeled underneath with the name of the month.

"What does *Ianuarius* mean?" I asked. I moved over beneath the arches and squinted as I looked up. My master lifted me up so I could see the square carving better.

The older Veronese boy answered the question before Dante could. "It's the name of this month, January, in Latin, the language of the ancient Romans. Does it look like January to you?"

The sculptor had pictured an old hooded man warming himself. I nodded. "I saw an old man just like that in the *piazza* today. His coat was thin and full of holes, and he sat by a fire to keep warm." *Februarius* showed a farmer venturing out into the cold to prune vines. "Remember, master? When we hiked north from Siena the grapevines looked like this."

Ser Dante's eyes traveled along the horizontal line above the arches, taking in each month. "I can feel the cold in my bones, just like the cold nights we knew in the mountains, Benito. This carver must have known the seasons in our mountains himself."

The figure for *Martius* stood blowing two large horns, suggesting strong winds. The older boy pointed to the horns. "When we act out March," he said, "we find curved tree branches to look like big horns. I guess the sculptor wanted us to think March announces itself with noisy winds."

Dante smiled. By *Aprilis* springtime had taken over, indicated by a woman wearing a warm coat but carrying two giant flowers. "Master, we saw flowers like this in the *Piazza delle Erbe* today, only they were dried ones."

"In April they will be real sunflowers," he replied, "but now in the winter the sunflowers for sale have been dried. The shopkeepers sell them for the oily seeds in the centers of the blossoms."

Maius was an armed warrior on horseback going out to battle with a shield and a lance.

"May is my favorite," said the tall boy. "When May comes around my friends and I pretend we are soldiers and carry on battles here in the piazza. Real horses are out on the farms, not here in the *piazza*, but our dogs play along with us and act like horses."

I began to think I was lucky to have Beffa tied up to a tree here, along with Galo. If I were in the game I'd have a real live donkey.

Iunius pictured a fruit-gatherer up in a tree with his basket. "Even I could do that," I said. "Then I wouldn't need a ladder, and I wouldn't need my master to lift me up. Is it hard to climb down the tree with a basket full of fruit?"

"My father tells me to practice by running up and down steps carrying a basket of apples," the older boy said. "I try to balance carefully because if the basket tips, the apples will be bruised and won't bring many *soldi* when we sell them in the market." I thought of the delicious dried peaches my master and I had eaten on the outskirts of Verona. They must have been picked like this too.

"Look, master, here is July, *Julius*, bending over to cut grain. Would my name in Latin be *Benitus* and yours be *Danteus*?" A laugh slid across Ser Dante's face as he pictured himself and me as Roman senators or gladiators. I would be a tiny Roman next to him!

"Now people speak Italian here," he replied, "and that is why I mostly write in Italian too, instead of Latin. Latin is a good language for many things, but if we want to speak with people around us we need to use their language."

"What happens in August?" I asked as his eyes moved along. "Oh, I see. The farmers, like my father used to do in the Casentino, have picked the grapes and now they want to make wine from them. So, they need barrels to put it in."

The carved figure for *Augustus* was busy hammering wine casks. Here were the barrels to store that delicious Soave and Valpolicella we had tasted in the *piazza*. "And here they are making the wine to put in the barrels," I continued, looking at September. "I could do this! This *tipo*, this fellow, has to do two things at once—pick the grapes with one hand and trample on them with his feet at the same time. Let me

down, Ser Dante, and I will try it." Jumping up and down on the pavement stones, I waved my arms wildly and reached for imaginary grape clusters in every direction.

"Here comes my little brother's favorite, the pig-fattening for October," the boy said. "He scurries around on the ground looking for pretend acorns that the rest of us pound off oak tree branches with long sticks." The bigger the hogs, the more delicious would be the bacon and the *prosciutto*. I thought of the *prosciutto Zia* Bianca wrapped around melon slices in the summer, and my mouth began to water.

"Your brother can't like November," I said to the boy. "Because then these big fat hogs have to die and be made into sausages for the winter. Look, the sculptor made one hog already hanging up and the other being killed. I wouldn't want to be a pig in November." Our eyes moved to the last carving, and Ser Dante saw the connection back to the January figure warming himself at a fire. Here, for December, workers were cutting and gathering firewood to warm themselves and their homes.

Later, my master told me that when he looked at the carvings he felt a warm swell of understanding, seeing this cycle so like those in the books he loved—the psalter and the poems—and so like the cycles in the countryside. Thinking back to his question about why the church portal didn't feature stories from the Bible, he realized that on the church entrance the calendar cycle justifiably took a rightful place. A church was supposed to remind worshippers about the wonder of all the created elements in the world, he told me, and to give them hope for better lives. The carvings bringing to life the rebirth of crops could bring comfort, reassuring churchgoers that the progression of the seasons would continue forever. Even though human life on earth was hard, especially when one had to endure harsh winters or landscapes like the mountains he and I had just come through, it followed an orderly and balanced rhythm.

Master Dante drew his eyes away from the lively sculptures to speak to the youth who had befriended them. "What is your name and where do you live?" Ser Dante asked.

"I am called Can Francesco della Scala," the boy replied, and my father Alberto was the lord of Verona until his death last year. My brothers Bartolomeo and Alboino and I were to share the ruling of the city, but since I am too young to govern yet, Bartolomeo now rules Verona. As *Signore di Verona* in the future, I welcome you to our home. My brother Bartolomeo always shelters travelers, as my father did before him. Look, you can just make out the outlines of our palace to the east along the river."

Master Dante rejoiced at our good fortune. He had been told by his Florentine friends that the della Scala family would be sympathetic to him in exile. He, our new young friend and I made our way to the court of the della Scalas.

CHAPTER NINE

Francesco was right about the welcome at his father's palace. "*Guardi*, look!" I exclaimed as we entered through the gate into the court yard. "*Com'è magnifico!*" My eyes widened as I stared at the carved doorways, the barred windows, and the elegant fountain. Can Francesco motioned to the Scaligeri groomsmen to lead Gagliardo and Beffa around to the stables in the rear, and ushered Dante and me into the first of several *salotti* or drawing rooms opening off to the right.

"*Tante grazie*, lad," Ser Dante said to Can Francesco, "we are most grateful."

A servant dressed in a velvet tunic brought in a tray with dried plums and wine, and indicated soft chairs where we might seat ourselves. Shortly, we were shown to our own rooms. Several apartments in the Scaligeri abode were set aside for the housing of visitors of many sorts, including artists, political figures, and clergy. Connected to the fine room for Dante was an antechamber supplied with a simple bed and wash basin, for me, his attendant Benito. We put down our wet heavy packs, pulled off our scarred boots, and sank into comfortable pillows. Using a pitcher of warm water and some soft cloths provided for us, we washed off our travelers' dust and put on clean tunics hanging for us in the wardrobe cabinets.

In Ser Dante's quarters the walls were decorated with scenes of changing fortune, both good and bad. The paintings showed Fortune as a woman, a goddess exercising her whims and balancing a scale, which tipped sometimes up and sometimes down for no particular reason. Some who had been kings became beggars, and some who had been chambermaids became princesses. "Can fortune be a person?" I asked. I had never thought so, but I knew people who changed their minds a lot. I felt like that when I worried if I had done the right thing to leave the Casentino and go with Ser Dante.

"Look, Benito," my master said, "we are not the only ones to suffer misfortunes. Even though we were forced to leave our homes and journey in the cold over the mountains, here we are in the company of our good lord Bartolomeo della Scala, who treats us like honored guests.

At dinnertime, washed and as well dressed as we could be, supplementing the poor clothing we had carried with us over the mountains with the elegant attire provided by our host, Ser Dante joined Bartolomeo and his other guests in a high-ceilinged banqueting room. Bartolomeo invited me to come too, and arranged for a place to be set for me in the kitchen with the scullery boys and the cooks. "*Che bello!*" I exclaimed as I smelled the delicious odors wafting from the fireplace in the warm kitchen. A big soup kettle hung over the coals, and the cooks ladled out steaming bowls of *linguini ai frutti di mare*, strips of pasta nestled in a seafood sauce.

"*Com'è gustoso*, how delicious!" I said.

"Our noble master's fishermen bring clams, eels and fish from the shallow waters of the Po River delta to the east," the master chef told me. "Our river, the Adige, turns southward toward the Po just east of Verona, and boats go back and forth often." I tucked a towel under my chin and dug in, remembering the skimpy meals of nuts and berries my master and I had called dinners during our trip over the mountains.

I peeked around the corner to see the grand *sala*. Ser Dante was seated facing an inner courtyard at the center of the Scala palace. Torches illuminated the tapestry-hung walls as servants brought in heaping platters of roast venison, savory simmered vegetables dried months earlier when they were harvested from the gardens, wild mushrooms and fennel and asparagus, warm bread, *risotto*, flagons of wine, and rich *castagnaccio*, a cake made from chestnut flour. Can Francesco's brother Bartolomeo and other members of the Scala family were dressed in brocades and furs, and a blazing fire in the huge stone fireplace kept everyone warm. Besides the servingmen there were musicians playing lyres and singing, jugglers, and jesters dressed in bright colors to entertain the lord and his guests. Friendly dogs roamed under the tables, gobbling up any delicacies that might drop to the floor. To my master it must have seemed a magical feast, after his days of cold and hunger trudging through the mountains.

After dinner Master Dante retired to his apartment, and I ran along behind him telling him everything that took place in the kitchen. "Master, they have a cook whose whole job is stirring the soup, and another one who doesn't do anything but cut the roast! And all the children of the cooks can eat as much as they want and they can start eating before everyone is served and...." Ser Dante interrupted me with a wave of his hand, noticing for the first time a writing desk, several quill pens, an inkstand, and paper, just for him. The sight of writing materials made his eyes gleam.

His wife Gemma, his children, his Florentine friends, and his beloved Florence were far away. He could never go home again, but at least his hosts in Verona knew that he was a writer and needed to write. Lighting a candle, he set to work, writing letters and ideas for verses, composing first in his head and then on paper.

Before his exile from Florence, my master told me, he had begun to formulate in his mind a long and complicated poem he called the *Commedia*. He could visualize the shape of his great poem, but for now he would write only little sections, to fit together in time. First he would have to get his footing in this life of exile. The next morning he told me that I fell asleep without even remembering to take off my tunic, and that before long the fatigue from the mountain hiking took its toll on him as well. He blew out the candle at his bedside and soon was asleep too.

Life at the Scaligeri court was sophisticated. Bartolomeo knew how to extend and strengthen the control his father had held over political factions in the Veneto, the area stretching alongside the Adige and Po rivers east toward Venice. To do that, he exercised a complicated system of patronage, hand in hand with luxurious hospitality. Writers and artists held positions of status at the Veronese court, so Ser Dante was provided with time and necessities to continue his work. To live at court, though, meant one had to take part in performances, dinners, and festivities. The extravagant life at court began to seem artificial for my master, too distant from his human roots. Here were the trappings of refined society, but without the earthy realities that he loved in his native Tuscany.

Life at court was never dull, but also never quite real. Sometimes the court jesters and astrologers were rude, but my master always felt that he must be polite and subservient out of deference to the great lords who had offered him temporary quarters. He was grateful to have a writing sanctuary, but his conscience dictated that he do the sort of writing that the Verona court requested, more than his own compositions. Since the Scaligeri had given him shelter, he repaid them by writing and delivering their diplomatic correspondence. On the rare occasions when he had time to spare, he invited our new friend, young Can Francesco, to visit with us in our rooms and to explore the streets of the city. We all became good friends as we admired the beautiful churches and squares in Verona.

"Master, visiting churches is fine, but sometimes I want Can Francesco to come out and play ball with me," I said when I caught glimpses of the young lord in my master's chambers.

"I must help my brothers, Benito," Can Francesco replied, although he didn't always seem happy about it. The young lord's activities were often tied to the opulent life at the Scaligeri court, and it was hard for him to break away.

"Master, why can't we have a dinner of bread and cheese like those at *Zia* Bianca's some time? And why do I always have to keep my clothes neat and clean? When can we go back out to San Zeno to play in the *piazza* there with Can Francesco and his friends and the kittens?" I asked.

"Ah, *è vero*, it's true, my boy," my master replied, "the courtly routine here can be wearing. But we must be thankful for the warmth, food, and clothing Bartolomeo and Alboino have been kind enough to give us. They will appreciate your helping clean the cupboards and floors in the kitchen, and we will go out to San Zeno again soon. Besides, the Scaligeri *capocuoco* who is in charge of the kitchen has promised to bake you a special *torta di mele*, apple cake, for your *compleanno* in a few days in early March. Reaching the age of eleven years is a milestone."

"I will gobble down the *torta*, and the kitchen workers are my friends. But most of the people who live and visit at court are stupid; they have *teste di cavolo*," I grumbled, calling the courtiers 'cabbage heads.' "They worry about fine clothes and they don't even like to play with *dadi*, dice."

"Be quiet. It is impolite to say such things about our hosts." Ser Dante hoped no one overheard my remark, but in truth he was tiring of court life himself. Living at the Scaligeri palace did not allow him enough time for his own writing.

Not long after, Can Francesco's brother Bartolomeo died, so Dante's young friend began to take on even more courtly responsibilities. After Bartolomeo's death Alboino succeeded to power. Master Dante found Alboino lacking in the nobility and compassion of his elder brother Bartolomeo.

"Master, can we get out of here?" I asked. "Even if I have to be cold and hike in the mountains again, I am sick of living like a fancy prince."

The time was right for my master to leave, and he agreed with me. The snows melted in February and we celebrated my birthday in early March. Later in the month we thanked our hosts, packed our few belongings and prepared to head back to the south once again, up into the mountains of the Casentino.

"I know we will find a monastery this time, master. The cook's helpers have been there and told me the way."

Ser Dante told me that the hospitality of the monks, although austere compared to that of the Veronese lords, would suit us, and would help him reconnect with the rhythms of the earth. With gratitude but hope in his heart for more peaceful surroundings, he said his goodbyes, especially to the young Can Francesco, who was growing into a handsome young man now called Can Grande, or the Great Hound. My master spoke for both of us. "Benito and I will come back,"

Dante told the youth, "and we will remember your great kindness. We will admire the panels of San Zeno again, and I will think about you and about the cycles of work the panels represent while we continue on our journey."

CHAPTER TEN

DESPITE the damp and the cold there was a spring to Ser Dante's walk as he and I headed back toward the mountains. "Look, Master," I said, pointing to the clouds in the sky to the southwest, "the birds are showing us the way." It was true. A pair of *falchi*, hawks, floated slowly up over the foothills, occasionally circling as they looked for mice or rabbits. Their graceful movements followed the curve of the rising hills, beckoning us to follow. I ran ahead, pulling Beffa along by his rope.

Crossing the flatlands along the river, Ser Dante and I gathered all the stray bits of grain we could find to fortify ourselves for the climb ahead. This time the Casentino had a familiar look. As we climbed higher, Ser Dante recognized some peaks and valleys that we had crossed before, when we were first exiled from Florence. "Here is a clear stream," he said, "let's stop and fill our water flasks. The creeks may still be frozen farther up the mountain."

"The water is so cold it makes my fingers ache!" I said. "And it's roaring down the mountain so fast! Does that mean the snow is melting up above? Might there be an avalanche?"

"It just means that we will not be thirsty, and that you must be careful about wading into the water. A torrent like this can knock you right off your feet and send you hurtling back down to Verona."

The thought of turning somersaults in a clear stream appealed to me, but I didn't say so to my master. Besides, doing somersaults would only be fun in the summer when I was hot and dusty. As we sat by the rivulet filling up our flasks and drinking the frosty water, my master thought of his beloved Arno River in Florence, into which the streams from the mountains flowed. He took out his quill and paper from his pack and wrote a few lines:

The streams which from the green hills
of Casentino flow down to the Arno,
making their beds cool and soft,

always stand before my eyes.

I interrupted his thoughts. My eyes had been busy darting around into the bushes in front of us. "I will pick some of these blackberries for our lunch, and beyond them there is a big tree full of *castagne*, chestnuts. They will fit in Beffa's pack and we can roast them for dinner." By now we knew how to provide for ourselves in rugged terrain, but my master might have overlooked the blackberries hidden in brambles. I could scramble under bushes more easily than he.

"*Grazie*. Your good eyes are a godsend to us."

"What is a 'godsend'?" I replied. "Do we need God to find food for us? Or is it my sharp eyes that find nuts and mushrooms, as you said?"

Dante chuckled. "Of course I depend on your eyes. It's just a way of speaking. *Chi s'aiuta, Dio l'aiuta*, God will help those who help themselves." As I scurried about picking up chestnuts under the tree, I imagined a big forest god dressed in fur, delivering rabbits and maybe even a deer or a wild goat to hungry hunters. Perhaps he would even rescue us from mountain pirates like the shaggy man who had awakened us before we got to Verona.

Later in the afternoon I did see an animal cross the path ahead of us, not more than thirty paces away. It wasn't a deer or a goat or a rabbit that we might have trapped for our dinner, but a menacing wolf. Turning its head toward us, it stopped and crouched down on its front paws, baring its teeth and growling. I jumped behind Master Dante, holding on to him as tightly as I could.

"Quiet," he whispered. "We mustn't show we are afraid or the wolf may attack." For several minutes we and the wolf stared at each other, Ser Dante standing tall and I still as a statue right behind him, with my arms around his hips. There was no noise other than the wolf's throaty growl and the scraping of its paw as it scratched the earth. My heart jumped into my mouth, paralyzing my tongue. The animal kept looking directly at us, its tail curved under its belly and its ears alert. It was as tall as I and mostly gray, with darker black ears and streaks of white fur. I could see scars on its back and one of its legs, where bumpy tufts of fur grew. It kept its head down, but I could see sharp fangs in its mouth.

Finally—it seemed like an hour to me but Ser Dante told me later it was only three minutes—the wolf stood up and turned its head, lifting its ears toward rustling noises in the brush. Just as quickly as it had appeared it arose and turned, moving quietly toward a cave under an overhang.

I could finally talk, though only in a whisper, as if I had been holding my breath for a long time. "Master, look!" I pointed. "There are two wolf cubs there, just beyond the clearing."

"No wonder the mother wolf threatened us," he said. "She feared we might hurt her babies. When she learned that we meant no harm, she retreated."

"Ser Dante, there must truly be a forest god, who will watch out for the *lupo mamma* and her babies too, as he looks after us."

"Walk quietly and stay away from their lair," Ser Dante cautioned. "The *padre lupo* must be nearby, and we mustn't let him think we are a danger to the *madre lupo* and the *bambini*." We turned our path in the direction away from the wolves' den, moving quietly and leading Galo and Beffa securely by the reins. We tried to walk silently, without making any sounds in the leafy carpet on the forest floor. Only after we were a good distance away and had seen no sign of the wolf family for nearly an hour did we stop to rest.

"I am proud of you," my master said. "You were as quiet as a *topolino*, a little mouse, and you let the *madre lupo* know we respected her and her babies. When we travel through the woods, we are visitors in the forest animals' home."

My heart was beating faster than usual, but I felt a new kinship with the mountain animals. They had to struggle to survive, and so did we. Questions for my master bounced around in my head. Once we made camp for the night and prepared a meager supper, we could talk.

"This is not the first time I have worked at not talking, master," I said. "When I asked my *Zia* Bianca too many questions while she was cutting the pasta into strips, she would tell me to close my mouth, saying *'In bocca chiusa non entrano mosche,'* no flies can get inside a closed mouth. Once I tried to eat flies when Pietro dared me, but I spit them out fast because they tasted awful." Ser Dante smiled and said I had learned well to be a silent forest walker, making no noise, breaking no branches, and leaving no tracks.

"You are a good helper, my boy." I lifted my chin a little higher, but I was happy the wolves were far behind us.

The next morning we took a different path toward the east, in hopes of finding the monastery Ser Dante knew was high up in these mountains. I liked to lead the climb, so I could scout out territory. As I clambered up a steep rise I came upon a small valley, pocketed amongst dense thickets of pine trees. Here there were patches of green where the snow had melted on the south sides of the slopes. "Master," I called, "I have found a good place for lunch. Shall we rest here?"

After we nibbled on the few *biscotti* in our knapsacks, I scampered ahead. Directly in front of us was a faint path. "Master! Master! There is a path here, without footprints of goats or wolves. People must have made it!" The path was crooked and hardly visible, but it was there, winding up and to the east. We followed it.

At the top of the next rise my master's hopes were rewarded. Across a sweeping valley we could barely see a *campanile*, surrounded by a cluster of low-lying simple stone buildings, lining a river. The rough slopes adjoining the structures had been leveled out a little, and plowed and planted.

"What's happening here?" I asked. "Are there people living in these mountains who plant gardens like my *Zia* Bianca*'s*? Maybe they grow juicy *carciofi*, artichokes, or at least some *cipolle*, onions that we can stir into our broth to make it taste better." Lately my mind had focused on eating.

Coming closer, we could see that the plots were vineyards, with rows of grapevines supported on wooden stakes. Three hooded figures moved about among the vines, not noticing that their work was being observed by mountain travelers. "Are they *fantasme*, ghosts, or real people, Ser Dante?" The distant figures did indeed look ghostlike, seeming to waft silently amid the rows of vines. They wore long woolen robes and were intently cutting back the longer grapevine branches with scythes that they carried either in one hand or tucked into the rope belts at their waists.

"They are monks," he replied. "Their hoods and their rope belts do give them an otherworldly look. But they are tending to their gardens just like your *Zia* Bianca does in the Casentino." Ser Dante knew they were pruning the vines so the *vendemmia* would bring larger and juicier grapes by the next summer. "Remember the panels at San Zeno? This is the work that the *agricoltori* do in the early spring, as in the February panel there."

He explained to me that March in the mountains was the time for preparing the vineyards in anticipation of a healthy crop. When the weather was still cold and most laborers stayed indoors sharpening axes and knives, a few braved the cold to ready the vines for another coming season. While they pruned the vines they could let out the lambs and goats to forage in the undergrowth for some early sprigs of green, without worrying that wolves or mountain lions would pounce.

"Benito, let's rest here, to be ready to greet our mountain comrades. We can watch them to learn what they are doing." I sat down on a flat rock, my mind swimming with ideas of hooded ghosts wandering about in planted fields with transparent sheep. Ser Dante took out his quill pen and added to his poetry notebook:

In that part of the young year
when the sun warms his locks beneath Aquarius
and the long nights are moving toward the south,

when the frost copies on the ground
the image of her white sister
although the point of her pen lasts but little,

the poor peasant whose fodder is getting low
rises, looks out, and sees the fields all white,
whereupon he strikes his thigh,

turns back and, lamenting, walks up and down
like a wretch who does not know what to do.
Later he looks out again and recovers hope

on seeing that the world, in a little while,
has changed appearance; and he takes his crook
and drives forth the lambs to feed.

I shook Ser Dante from his poetic reverie. "Master, look! They have spotted us and are looking our way."

My master and I made our way down the slope until Ser Dante was near enough to call to the workers: "*Buon giorno, signori!*" Two of the men stopped for a moment and looked up, regarding us with penetrating gazes, but they said nothing and soon returned to their work. The third, however, stood up straight, put down his scythe, and extended his hand to my master.

"*Benvenuto*," he said quietly as he addressed us. "We are Benedictine monks here, and have taken vows of silence, so my comrades cannot address you. Because I am an abbot I have the privilege of welcoming the few strangers or pilgrims who venture up this high in the Casentino, especially in the chill of early spring. We are honored by your presence, and you are welcome to stay if you like. There are extra cells for sleeping, and our fare is simple but nourishing. If you are ill, we have built a hospital here, next to the church. This place is called Camaldoli, but originally we called it *Fontebona* because of the abundance of good water here. It is a pleasant place. The name Camaldoli comes from the words '*Campo Amabile*,' or 'lovely meadow'."

I tugged at Ser Dante's cloak and huddled closer to Beffa's soft belly. "What is he talking about, master? He sounds like the friar at *Zia* Bianca*'s* little church at home."

"Hush," Dante said, turning his attention back to the monk. "*Grazie*, we are weary from traveling and we welcome your offer of hospitality."

CHAPTER ELEVEN

THE abbot accompanied us up the vineyard slope until we all arrived at a small paved entry *piazza* near the bell tower. "Before we go in we must stop and pray together," said the abbot, "because the bell will soon be ringing for *tierce*, one of the eight hours dedicated each day to prayer by all the brothers."

I wished we could find a place to have a nap first, because the mountain travel had made me tired, but I could tell that Ser Dante intended for us to do exactly as the monk had directed. After the bells and the communal prayer, the abbot escorted us to the monks' dormitory, where Ser Dante and I were each assigned a square stone cell equipped with a simple bed. For washing, there was a pitcher, placed on a bench made from a tree trunk.

"Signor Dante," the abbot said, "although we live frugally here we do accommodate guests, especially those who worship as we do and who respect our quiet way of life here in the mountains. We are honored by your visit."

"Ser Dante," I whispered, "shall I go back to my mountain routine of not opening my mouth and being as quiet as I possibly can? I am very good at it now."

"*Sí, silenzio*. We will do as the monks do, and follow their rules about eating, talking, praying, and sleeping."

The abbot informed my master that the main meal was to be at *none*, roughly six in the afternoon, and that of the eight prayer hours each day, the first was to be at Vigils or Matins, between midnight and two in the morning, followed by Lauds at daybreak. Vespers came at sundown, followed by Compline, after which no one was to speak. Except for prayers, the bulk of the day was to be devoted to manual labor, since the monks believed in communal work, obedience, study, and the denial of unnecessary luxury.

"Why are there so many rules?" I asked. Ser Dante explained that all activities at the monastery were to be done at the designated hours, as regulated by the bells. A fulfilled and successful life for each participant would create a fulfilled and successful life for the whole community. Still, there was some leeway. Consideration was given to each monk's basic personal needs and to the practical necessities of living an isolated and self-sufficient life high up in the mountains. Each monk was allowed a *hemina*, one fourth of a liter, of wine per day, and brothers who were working in fields distant from the monastery could pray there rather than journey back to the main church. Two cooked meals were served each day, and spiritual readings took place in the morning and evening, before and after manual labor. I listened to my master, but life at the monastery still didn't seem like much fun, and there weren't any children to play with.

"Perhaps," Ser Dante whispered, "this way of life may suit us better than that at the court of Can Grande in Verona. There was much idle feasting there, and many of the courtiers cared more about elegant clothes and servants than about work and friendship."

"But," I whispered back, "didn't you like feasting just a little bit? My stomach is growling!"

"Life here is both poorer and richer," Ser Dante replied. "We will eat enough and we will enjoy peace and quiet. I can do my own work and the two of us can help the monks with their work as well."

I thought about what my master had said. Perhaps life here would be like that at my *Zia* Bianca's, except without friends to play with. At least the planting and the caring for animals would be the same, and I would like that.

Activity at the monastery was shaped by the seasons of the year and the seasons of the church, in accordance with recurring human activities. In Dante's mind such a plan offered hope and stability, because human lives fit comfortably into rhythmic patterns regulated by the earth's cycles as well as by the church's cycles. "Benito, you and I can live here for a while in peace," he said. "You can care for Gagliardo and Beffa and help with the lambs and the goats, and I can tend to my writing."

At Camaldoli the mountain itself embodied serenity and continuity, and the orderly life of the monks living there magnified that peaceful state. After my master and I had washed ourselves and eaten our simple meal, Ser Dante took up his quill again and noted an idea:

The holiness of the mountain cannot manifest itself without order.

Though he had welcomed the gaiety and intelligence of the Scaligeri court in Verona, he knew that to write meaningful poetry he needed quiet.

The next morning I fed Beffa and Galo and walked out to the goat pen, where I could see the monks feeding and grooming the animals. I smiled at them and began to help, and they smiled back in return. We do not even have to talk to one another to be friends, I thought! When the bells indicated it was time for prayers, I followed my new friends into the chapel and then back out again to the vineyards, where I found that I could help them greatly because I was short enough to climb under the grape trellises to tie up the vines. On our way back from the vineyards the youngest monk picked me up and sat me on his shoulder. I hugged him and smiled.

The snow melted in the mountains. The brothers celebrated the return of their lord at Easter, and green shoots reappeared through the layers of brown leaves under the trees. Violets, crocuses and the delicate *biancospino* or white hawthorn now sparkled on the slopes. The brothers left their heavy cloaks in their cells and took to digging trenches for vegetable planting in the fields near the vineyards. They corralled their herds and sheared their sheep of thick winter coats to ready the wool for carding, spinning, and weaving.

As spring approached, nights were clear on the mountaintops so that the stars seemed more brilliant and nearer than they had appeared down in the villages. Ser Dante and I watched as the constellations seemed to move in their orbits higher and higher as the months went forward. "The earth has its order and the sky its own order too," he said. "The two paths work together and become one. It is a tandem path, that of the annual movement of the sun and that of the succession of the months."

I liked watching the stars at night with Ser Dante. We were close and warm together, and I tried to think big thoughts about the movements of the sun and the earth, and the months becoming warmer. "Why do you think that the earth moves?" I asked. "I don't feel it moving underneath me."

"You can watch the stars," he replied. "Each month they appear to be in a slightly different part of the sky, even though we look at them at the same time of night from the same place."

Then Ser Dante took a stick and drew a picture for me in the dirt of the big round earth. In bigger circles around it he drew the heavens, with many stars. "Imagine," he said, "if we lived on the other side of this earth we would see a whole different group of stars in other formations."

I tried to picture all that but my head grew fuzzy and I rested it against Ser Dante's shoulder. "You think about such big ideas," I said. "Maybe my ideas are still small because I am small. But will I learn?"

"Benito," he said, "you are bright and you will learn. And your children and grandchildren will learn even more. The world is there for us to learn about." I smiled and curled into his shoulder.

"Have the bells rung for us to go to bed yet, Master?" I said sleepily.

The next day Ser Dante continued our conversation under the stars by telling me about the signs of the zodiac. Once in Verona, a traveler had approached us as we sat in the piazza facing San Zeno with Can Francesco, talking about the cycles of work carved there. In some churches, he said, in addition to the monthly labors, sculptors had included the signs of the zodiac. "What does 'zodiac' mean?" I asked.

"The word 'zodiac' refers to divisions among the heavens, whose names and symbols are suggested by the arrangement of stars in that part of the sky," he said. "Remember when I read to you the lines of poetry I wrote earlier beginning with:

'In that part of the young year
when the sun warms his locks beneath Aquarius
and the long nights are moving toward the south'?

"I was writing about Aquarius, the sign of the zodiac which governs the period from late January until mid-February. We usually picture Aquarius as a water-bearer, a man carrying a jug of water."

"Sometimes," he continued, "sculptors carve only the signs of the zodiac rather than the labors of the months, and sometimes they picture the zodiac signs and the labors together."

"Does the jug of water mean that in February the snow is melting?" I asked. "What are some other signs, and do they show what happens in other months too?"

"You can look at it that way," he said. "Pisces the fish stands for part of March, Taurus the bull for part of May, and Leo the lion for part of August. Do you think those signs might tell us something about those months?"

I thought about the fish and the bull and the lion. "Well, Aquarius brings water in February and after it comes Pisces, a fish to swim in the water." Ser Dante smiled. "But I'm not sure about the bull in May and the lion in August, unless spring bursts in like a bull and the heat of summer roars like a lion."

He chuckled. "You are starting to think like a poet. Poets have to imagine pictures in their heads and then write about them. What you are talking about are symbols."

"What is a symbol?" I asked. Thinking about the stars and the zodiac and symbols was stretching my head till it ached.

"It's easy. A symbol is just an idea or a picture that stands for something else. For instance, a picture of a flop-eared donkey could stand for Beffa, or—as you suggested—a porcupine could stand for the spiky towers of the town of San Gimignano. Or even the image of you being carried back to the monastery by the smiling monk could stand for friendship."

I began to believe that thinking like a poet might be something I could do. "*Bene*," I said to him. "But I would feel even more poetic if we built a castle out of these rocks, and then went inside for some soup."

We stayed at the monastery for a few more weeks, and I learned that my master's ideas made sense. He told me that dividing up the calendar into the months of the zodiac and the labors of the months gave him a window into the immensity of time. Initially, time had seemed to him like a big ocean with never-ending waves, but thinking of it as divided up in natural segments—like spring and summer and autumn and winter—made sense. We couldn't capture time, or stop it in its tracks, but we could tame it a little by adapting our chores to its natural rhythms.

By the time April rolled in, the monks moved from pruning to planting and wool preparing. We were isolated here on top of the world, and our lives depended on patterns of working with plants and animals.

"Do you think *Zia* Bianca has begun to shear her sheep yet?" I asked as the days warmed.

"You are thinking of home," he said. "I think of it too, and I ache for the family and the work I had to leave behind in Florence."

"Will we go down the mountain again soon, Ser Dante?" I asked. "You and I are good travelers, even if we can't go home again." He smiled at me and put his arm around my shoulder, which was growing bigger and stronger from all my work helping the monks.

"We will go together," he said. "Perhaps you will grow into a poet, or at least a person with visions. If one has big ideas one can make a difference in the world."

"Master, sometimes I just like to think of little ideas like rabbits or dinner or a clean tunic, but up here I have tried to stretch my brain by thinking of big ones too."

Ser Dante smiled the smile I had come to know as meaning he appreciated what I had said or done. "From this vantage point up on the mountain, you and I have experienced not just the world people can see and hear and touch, but also that imagined invisible world in the sky and the heavens."

I tried to corral ideas about work and stars, which seemed like seeds Ser Dante had sowed in my head. Maybe they would grow into something in time. The monks were my friends, but I missed playing with other children. "You have given me many ideas to think about, Master. But the trail is calling us too. Look, there are wildflowers blooming by the path."

Ser Dante took my hand and we led Beffa and Gagliardo back down the mountain. He would seek once again the company of men committed to the busy needs of learning and politics and trade, and I was eager for new adventures. Our good friends the brothers at Camaldoli packed our knapsacks with cheese and biscuits and dried fruit, and we began walking again, this time down a mountain slope never before explored.

CHAPTER TWELVE

WE settled in walking to the south, following the path of the sun, into rock outcroppings. I found a branch from a fir tree that served as a walking stick when we had to dismount and lead Beffa and Gagliardo. As we climbed downward we reached a thickly wooded valley where the dense treetops hardly admitted any light.

"How do we know where we are headed?" I asked. On our first two mountain hikes we were looking first for Verona, and then for a monastery, but after leaving Camaldoli our direction seemed uncertain. Something inside me wanted to know answers, but I mostly had questions.

"We have to do the best we can and leave some matters to chance," my master replied. "I know we are strong travelers, and I believe in good fortune." Talking about fortune reminded me of the painted walls at the Scaligeri palace in Verona, where Lady Fortune's scales sometimes tipped up and sometimes tipped down. It wasn't a comforting thought. I was eleven now. Shouldn't I begin to be able to control directions in my life? How could I learn to accept matters calmly, as Ser Dante did?

It was still murky under the forest canopy when we stopped for our noonday rest. Ser Dante wrote some lines of verse in his notes, and when he read them to me later I knew that he too was not sure how we would find our way, even though he had tried to be positive when he spoke to me.

In the middle of the journey of our life
I came to my senses in a dark forest,
for I had lost the straight path.

"Why do you call this the 'journey of our life,' Master?"

"I can't describe exactly why yet," he said, "but I feel that you and I are exploring something bigger than these Apennine Mountains. Eventually we may find clues about how humans should live their lives everywhere, rather than just about how you and I should live. I worked to bring about good government in Florence, and I believe that most people can be just and good to one another. But sometimes temptations to do bad things draw our brothers and sisters away from being good."

"Like those horrible black Guelphs, Master!"

"Yes. They are among the worst." His face darkened as the memory of losing his home and family back in Florence took over his mind. He told me he sometimes thought of storming back to avenge wrongs, but when he remembered the death sentence on his head should he enter the city, he realized he could not. People must learn to accept some things they couldn't change, he said. I wasn't so sure, because I wanted to change lots of things, especially getting back at mean people like that scary man in the mountains.

"What makes people hurt each other, Ser Dante?"

"Different reasons. Sometimes people are greedy for power or money or fame, like the black Guelphs. Sometimes they are just vain and silly, like some of the courtiers in Verona. Hurts can be big or little."

"It's hard to be good all the time, but at least I can try not to be bad. I can practice by being good to the animals and birds living in these woods, as you taught me to do on the way to Camaldoli," I said.

"*Certo*. We learn to be better, too, when we take responsibility for what we do, as you learned in your midnight horse race in Rome." I blushed, thinking that perhaps my master had forgotten about that by now. He was right, though. I needed to accept his criticism and move on.

"I am learning from you and I like that," I said, "but I miss my old life too. *Zia* Bianca made me work hard but she took good care of me, and I had friends to play with. Are you sure we can never go back?"

"Well, Benito, you and I work hard too, and we also are caring for each other. But my enemies will kill me and kill you too if we ever go back into Florence. You will make friends in other places. I like friends and playing too," he said. "Sometimes through play we can learn how to act when life is rough. I used to play pretend war, but when I grew up I fought real battles and made both true enemies and true friends."

I thought I would rather have true friends than true enemies, but maybe something good could come from war. I needed to think about it more. How could someone grow from having scary adventures?

As we rested on some moss under the tree branches, Ser Dante told me a story about friendship and bravery. He said that as a boy he had loved to climb in the mountains behind Florence, especially to his favorite hill near the green and white church of San Miniato. Once he had tried to hike even farther, clambering uphill in ravines more and more engulfed with brambles until the path disappeared altogether and the overhanging rocks allowed no entrance. He had shivered, hearing the squawking cries of birds over his head and the rustling of claws of strange animals in the heavy vegetation to his left and his right. Meeting this impasse, he had turned around to make his way back to his home. The wilderness above was frightening and fierce for a boy hiking alone. When he reached his house and told his family of his fears, his grandfather Bellincione had picked him up in his arms and cradled him.

"Dante," Bellincione told my master, "I myself tried to hike past San Miniato several months ago, and I can't make my way up there either. I am too old to make the climb, just as you are too young to do it. There is a season for everything, and soon you will be strong enough to conquer any mountain range, before you reach old age like me and cannot manage it anymore. That will be the time for you to sit in the shade, play with your cats and dogs, and remember how you learned to overcome difficult challenges in your life."

My master told me that he had thought about his grandfather's words as he sat comfortably in the old man's lap. He noticed that as his grandfather grew older, he couldn't walk as well or see as well as he could when he was younger, even though his mind and his heart were as clear and warm as ever.

"Human lives have cycles too," Ser Dante said. "We have seen the stars circling in the heavens, and work repeating itself in the fields, and the seasons of the church follow one another at the monastery in Camaldoli. Growing from infancy to adulthood is like this too, a cycle like the cycles of the heavens and the church and of human work. When I was young I struggled to climb these mountains, but now you and I can do it. When I was a child, I assumed that Florence would be my home forever, but now I can never go back. If life is really a cycle, then some happiness will come to us eventually."

I listened to my master and understood some of what he said. I understood how comforting a father or grandfather could be, and how old people and children were somehow alike. But I was still confused about cycles. Sometimes Ser Dante used too many words. Maybe that was what poets did. It was clear, though, that my master, like his grandfather, had a big heart. He wanted to believe the best. I hoped for the best too, but I still worried about that goddess with her scales tipping downward.

Since my head was swimming with words, I needed to do something instead of think, so I got up to see what was on top of the rock ridge behind us. I found footprints in the snow. "Master! Do mountain lions live up here? Or maybe wolves? Or maybe monsters? Giovanni told me once in the Casentino that a one-eyed monster with huge claws for feet lived in a cave up here and liked to eat little boys. Did he and Pietro and Iacopo and Antonia hear that from you?"

"No, Benito, Giovanni has a big imagination. If it is a mountain lion he will be more afraid of us than we are of him, and if it is a wolf it is probably bringing food to wolf babies on the other side of this peak that the Benedictines call Falterona. But animal tracks can help us find the best way down from these mountaintops."

We worked our way along the steep ledges and through dense undergrowth, following the tracks to see how the bed of the Arno River would grow stronger and wider as it rushed south toward Florence. "After the river rushes south to Florence it curves to the west and meanders toward Pisa, covering more than a hundred miles till it reaches the sea." He took out his quill and wrote three more lines of poetry:

Through the center of Tuscany
a little stream flows that rises in Falterona,
and a hundred miles are not enough for its course.

The flinty heights of Falterona were steep. I scraped my knees until they bled, and we both took a tumble on slippery snow once, saving ourselves from sliding into the icy stream only by grabbing a tree stump jutting out over the water. Beffa and Galo managed the best they could, but they were stumbling too. Once or twice we followed a narrow creek bed in hopes of finding a smooth path down, only to discover that the stream ended in a rushing waterfall too steep for us to descend. The melting March ice cracked and hurtled toward the lower slopes, carrying the water crashing down toward Florence.

"Master, you won't believe the huge waterfall I saw! This must be the monster of the mountain, not the one-eyed one Giovanni told me about!" I shouted as I made my way back to where he and the animals were struggling along the rocky path.

"I believe you, because I can hardly hear what you are saying, with the pounding noise it is making."

We both stopped talking as the thundering noise filled the wilderness. Careful to hold on to tree branches to avoid falling, we moved closer. The enormous waterfall cascaded precipitously from one rock plateau to another, zigzagging down the mountain with such force that no person could have kept his footing if he ventured into it. Its noise was deafening. My master found a safe footing, perched on a low log, and wrote in his notes:

Already I had reached a place where the roar
of the water falling into the next circle
could be heard, like the hum of a beehive,

"Have you ever heard of a waterfall this big, Master?" I asked Ser Dante.

"I hear that people call it the Aquacheta," he replied, "but I have never seen it before and I did not imagine it could be so powerful." We looked across from the clearing in the forest where we sat, midway down the cascading levels, to the other side.

"There are buildings over there, Master! I can barely see them through the mist of the falls, but they are there, a little higher than where we are."

My master squinted and looked through the watery mist. "It could be a mill by the bank of the river. Maybe the mountain dwellers there have learned to harness the waterfall's power for grinding grain. If it is a mill, we are fortunate, because activity like that suggests a community."

"But Master, we can never cross over this fierce stream."

"True. We must stay on this side of the waterfall and look for another way. But at least we know that other men have been near here, and may even be near here now." My legs were cold and tired as we turned our steps back through the forest, looking for another way to reach a place where people were living or might have lived. We had left Camaldoli in April, just after the month of March with its stinging and pelting winds, and now we used all our strength to keep from being blown over stone ledges into the deep canyons below.

After we reached a hollow of relative safety away from the ledge, my master talked with me about wind. Maybe he thought that talking about it would make me feel better in our cold and dangerous situation.

"Benito, there may be a great wind god in the sky blowing mercilessly, like the figure blowing two horns on the San Zeno doors. Or nature itself might be the wind god, blowing mercilessly up here in the mountains in March and April."

I shivered. "Whatever it is, I don't want any more of it. My fingers are freezing."

"But after March and April comes May, so spring can't be far away," he said. I wished I could be as cheerful as he, but thinking ahead was hard.

Following the wind came a heavy fog, advancing down the mountain and enveloping everything in its wet darkness. I huddled close to the animals. "Beffa," I whispered into his cocked ear, "I trust you. If we get lost forever in the fog, take me down to safety with you." Beffa whinnied, and I rubbed his warm nose. Since my master and I couldn't see to walk any farther, he sat down and wrote:

> *Reader . . . in the mountains a mist*
> *has caught you, through which your sight*
> *was like a mole's, through a membrane.*

I had to ask him what a membrane was, but I understood when he described it as a thin piece of stretched sheepskin. You could see light and shapes through it, but not make out clear outlines.

There was no choice; we had to stop and make camp for the night. At dawn we awoke to see a cleansed sky, a welcome sight for anyone and especially for pilgrims hiking through the mountains.

CHAPTER THIRTEEN

"MASTER," I shouted as I emerged from a clump of tall trees, "I think I see a bell tower!"

"I count on your eyes. Let me look too. Yes, it may be a pinkish brick building."

We made our way closer. Coming near, we saw that the tower belonged to a tiny church appearing to hang in space, glued to the mountainside behind it. It sat in the midst of a small settlement. Clambering through the vines and underbrush, at the top of a steep flight of stairs hugging the hillside we at last reached the church with its simple rounded entryway. A carving identified the place as San Godenzo.

"*Ahi,* I know this place!" my master said. "I signed a pact here, in this church, with some other Guelph leaders, when we were trying to reconcile political differences." I wondered why leaders would meet in hidden places in the mountains, but I hesitated to question my master. He continued: "We have gotten to the Mugello, a region in the Sieve River valley to the west of the Arno. Even though we appear to be buried in green mountain valleys, we are just a short distance from the Alighieri lands in Pagnolle in the Casentino."

"My *Zia* Bianca and my cousins may be less than a day's climb away!"

"Yes, my son. But it is not safe for us to go there."

My face fell. I had hoped to surprise *Zia* Bianca and my cousins, so we could hug each other, eat fresh apples, and play in the barn. But my master was right. The cruel black Guelphs would be waiting there for us, thinking I might try to hide with my family. I had thrown in my lot with Ser Dante and I had to choose him over my aunt and my cousins, so I said nothing.

"My friends have told me that there are other mountain palaces near here where we will be welcome and safe," my master said. "I have heard that the Guidi rulers who have mountain fortresses here are compassionate peacemakers."

As we walked along he told me about some of the fortified strongholds—Porciano, Romena, and Poppi. The names sounded like a song to me, so I chanted them in a makeshift melody as we walked, after my master stopped to pray once again in the peaceful chapel of the church in San Godenzo.

"Porci, Poppena, Romiano, here we come," I hummed, ignoring my master's corrections about my having the names all wrong. They sounded better in my song the way I sang it, and I liked singing in the mist and rain.

Since my master knew about the Sieve River valley, he realized we needed to curve back again toward the east, around Monte Falterona and back toward Camaldoli, but now on a lower level.

"Must we hike through more wind and ice?" I asked.

"As we descend, we will be warmer, because the northern *tramontana* wind won't reach us. We will hunt for a flat mountain ridge, a place called Pratomagno. *Prato* means meadow and *magno* means big, but it's not really a meadow. If we can find it I will know how to reach one of the castle fortresses. To make sure we keep moving to the east we must watch the shadows, to see from which direction sunlight comes."

I remembered the shadow games I had played in Pagnolle, seeing how our own shadows were tiny at noon and grew longer in the late afternoon. "But master, how can we watch shadows when the weather is stormy? Maybe we will end up in Africa instead."

"You are right about the sun and the shadows. But you are wrong about Africa. It is far away from here, across a big sea. To let the shadows help us find our way, we will wait out the wind and rain."

We found cover beneath a craggy overhang. The dark wetness made a piercing impression on my master, as he wrote:

You know how the air collects
the vapor which turns to water
when it rises to where cold condenses it.

When day was spent he covered the valley
from Pratomagno to the great mountain range
with clouds and made the sky above dark,

so that the saturated air turned to water.
The rain fell, and what the land
could not absorb ran to the ditches,

and as the water formed great streams
it rushed in such a torrent to the royal river
that nothing could hold it back.

I decided I might not want to be a poet, because writing verses beneath a cold rock while freezing rain poured in sheets in front of us didn't seem like fun to me.

"Master," I asked at last, "how can you write when it is so cold and damp and we have no place to go?"

At first he seemed not to hear me because he was so engrossed in shaping the words, but at last he said, "Writing can make me ignore such difficulties, because it takes me into another world that I invent."

I thought about what he had said and tried to stretch my ideas. If I became a writer like my master, I might write about parades or feasts like that at *Natale*, Christmas. Then I could transport myself right into the middle of them, and feel warm and happy and loved instead of cold and sad and alone! Writing did have power.

We waited beneath the sheltering rock, watching sheets of water roar past us. Gradually the torrent became lighter as the storm abated and the cascade thinned to droplets through which we could see sparkling bits of sunshine. "Master, we can walk down from here now! The rain is over and I want to hunt for this place called Pratomagno." It was still cold, but we forced our toes into freezing crevices and held on to tree roots for support as we climbed down and to the east.

At last, as we rounded a cliff we saw the shape of a building . . . yes, a castle, just as my master had hoped! "We are near the Pratomagno," he said. "Thirteen years ago I was in a great battle here, on the plain of Campaldino below. The castle is called Poppi, and it is one of the mountain strongholds of the Guidi counts."

"Did people die in the battle?" I asked. Battles sounded exciting but scary, and I was still not sure that anything good could come from them.

"I was very young then, my son. The Florentines and their neighbors from Arezzo fought fiercely and I saw a lot of blood." His voice became a whisper. "Too many people died, Benito, too many people. The Florentines won, but the cost was great. We flew our victory flag from the tower of that castle over there, but my heart ached. At least, a time of peace followed."

From our distant mountain perch the castle looked like a doll's house to me, perched at the top of a tiny town. I was eager to reach it, but to get there we had to hike down into the valley and then back up. "If we keep watching the tower, we will get there faster," I said, but even so we walked more than another hour before drawing close. Finally, the building's imposing outline began to emerge. We reached the foot of the hill, crossed a stream, and began climbing up the crooked streets of the town below the castle. It was still high above us, but we could see its outline more clearly over the rooftops.

"Why is the castle top so jagged?" I asked.

"Those rectangular openings make safe places for archers to defend the castle," he said. "Guards patrolling those ramparts would have a clear view of anyone foolhardy enough to besiege such a fortress, since their crossbows could easily pick off attackers." The idea of fighting began to appeal to me more. If I were defending the castle I would be safe behind the brick walls. But what if I were the attacker?

Suddenly I realized that maybe those people inside would think my master and I were attackers. "What happens if friendly people come to the castle, but those inside think those approaching are unfriendly?"

"We will approach with care and make our good wishes known."

Still not certain of our reception, we remained hidden by the thick branches of trees adjoining the small square facing the castle at the top of the hill. But as we peered out from behind the leaves, I burst into a smile. "They are having a *festa*! I don't see any guards at all, only people singing and dancing in front of the castle."

In the small piazza before the entryway were ten or twelve *contadini*, country people, dressed in mountain clothes, tunics made of deerskin. Some trailed banners of bright curling fabric while others played pipes and tambourines. "I was thinking about parades and now we have found one!" I exclaimed. "Can I go and dance too?"

The spots of color and the lively music contrasted sharply with the austere brick tower over the castle's entryway where the portal guard stood, blowing an impressive horn. Like the windy March horn, this one trumpeted the joyful return of spring color, but to the walls of the castle courtyard rather than to the forest floor. As the snow began to melt, it was time to decorate the castle inside and out with shields and banners.

"Can I try to blow your horn?" I asked the castle horn blower, who looked like the one carved on the church at San Zeno. "Why is everyone dressed up and why are they singing?"

"You may try, but it is hard to blow even for a grown man. Here, try blowing into this opening." My face turned red but no noise came out of the horn. "We are celebrating because the spring winds are coming, reminding mountain dwellers that they can soon return to the fields to dig for spring planting and to prune grape vines."

My master's face wore a smile too. "This is a time for celebration, and the bright colors and music reflect renewed vigor in the fields and vineyards." Here at Poppi the patterns of agriculture and the advancing of the seasons were coming to life in a festival of rebirth. My master knew he had found a happy place for us.

I held Ser Dante's hand and we joined the singing and swirling thread of dancers winding their way around the castle entry, and into the atrium and courtyard, where we found rough wood tables piled high with wine, dried fruit, nuts, and cheeses. Carried along in the midst of the happy throng, we passed under an archway decorated with shields. The castle atrium was protected by three-story high brick walls, reinforced by a double row of wooden balconies. Safely within the walls, I forgot about the ice and snow and cold on the mountains outside. In the center of the fortress, surrounded on four sides by protecting ramparts, everyone was safe.

"Who is that on the big throne over there?" I asked, looking at a man seated on a thick stone dais at one end of the inner courtyard.

"He is the Guidi ruler," Ser Dante replied, "the lord of this castle." The lord's ruddy face was smiling as he looked over the jostling crowd. A massive stone staircase led upward, eventually turning to the left beneath frescoed wall paintings. The stone walls behind the dais and next to the stairway were studded with coats of arms of the Guidi family and their relatives and friends.

The rough appearance of the castle reminded me that it was really a fortress, and that I had been right to worry as we approached from the mountains. But today there were no battles except mine as I chased the dog that had grabbed my sausage and run under the table. "Ser Dante, I like this *festa* much better than the fancy ones in Verona at the court of the Scaligeri. Down there, I had to think about being on good behavior all the time."

"There is much truth in what you say. It is good that everyone celebrates together, and that you do not have to eat in the kitchen with the servants." We all sat at simple tables made of hewn wooden planks, serving ourselves with hefty helpings of thick *ribollita*, a hearty soup, and chunks of crusty unsalted Tuscan bread. The horn blower escorted Dante to the dais and presented him to the Guidi ruler, who welcomed us with gusto.

"*Benvenuto* to our festival. You must stay and feast with us today to welcome the beginning of spring," he said, "you look walk-weary, tired, and hungry." My master and I put down our packs on a pile of straw behind the benches along the tables. I scurried outside to make sure Beffa and Gagliardo were tethered and fed, and then rushed back to stuff handfuls of the savory food into my mouth. I felt at home right away here. Something about the Guidi mountain people reminded me of my *Zia* Bianca and my friends in Pagnolle.

Before we fell asleep later that night, my master told me that he felt welcome too.

"I like these sturdy people, because they do not pretend to be anything they are not. They are genuinely glad to have us here, like the monks at Camaldoli."

"I like it better than Camaldoli, because here I can make all the noise I want." For whatever reasons, both my master and I, cut off from our families in Florence and in the Casentino, felt we were joining a new family. Spring at Poppi was blustery but bursting with new possibilities.

CHAPTER FOURTEEN

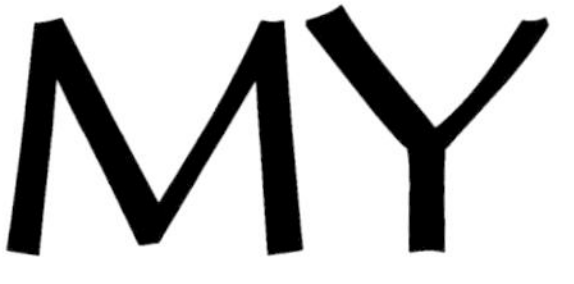
master and I stayed at Poppi until all the winter snow had melted and spring flowers began to bloom. Many of the Guidi family members living either in the castle or nearby in the town had children, and after I had seen to my duties with Beffa and Galo I was free to play. The count's grandson Alessandro taught me to play *bilie*, marbles, and on warmer days he and I took Beffa and explored the Campaldino plain at the bottom of the hill. We pretended we were warriors in the battle Ser Dante had told me about. "*Ahi,* Alesssandro, you'll never find me over here!" I shouted as I ran for cover and buried my face in tall grasses. Even though our play didn't include real fighting and real blood, like Ser Dante had encountered, I couldn't entirely get those ideas out of my mind.

While we played at fighting, my master wrote diplomatic letters for the Guidi dukes and counts, and questioned everyone about what might be happening down in Florence. Couriers came and went from Poppi to other castles and strongholds in northern Italy, delivering messages to the Guidi ruler and also taking copies of Ser Dante's writings to distribute. Word was filtering back to him that his poem was widely read, despite the knowledge that a death sentence loomed over his head back in Florence.

"Are you sad to hear news of your old home, when we cannot go there?" I asked him.

His eyes misted a little but his voice was strong. "I always long for news of my friends and my family, Benito, and I have heard that Gemma, Giovanni, Pietro, Jacopo, and Antonia are well, as is your *Zia* Bianca. But the black Guelphs still control the city, so the Florentines are not free. I long to help, but I can do so only through my writing." The sadness in his voice made me sad too. Exile wasn't fair!

Still, life held promise. April was the month for rebirth, new beginnings, and the return of blossoming beauty. The earth had stretched its muscles a little in February and more in March, and by April there was no denying the coming of spring. As the mountainsides came alive with carpets of red and yellow and orange and violet, Ser Dante spoke to me about the stout woman in the April San Zeno panels.

"Remember her? She carried a big flower and stood between two leafy trees, as if she were carrying two giant blossoms."

"We are looking at flowers like that all around us, Master," I said. "Just look to the south there, beyond the wall."

Ser Dante's voice was wistful as he replied, "Yes, the flowers lead us back down to Tuscany."

I could tell that my master was anxious to be traveling again. The Guidis urged us to stay and offered my master a quiet place to write, but he wanted to journey closer to his home city. Now the trek down the mountains would be easy, without the ice of January, the cold of February, and the blustery winds of March. On the day when we were preparing our travel packs he told me that hope kept welling up in his breast, telling him that maybe—just maybe—the political winds had subsided too, and he could one day return to his native Florence.

"I hope so. I want you to be happy," I said, but my heart was not as hopeful as my words. I remembered the threats that Ser Dante and I would be murdered if we ever ventured back into Florence, and I shivered at the thought.

We set off toward the south, following the curve of the ever-widening Arno River first to the east and then back to the west and the north toward the city of my master's birth. "Even if we are still banned from entering Florence," he said, "perhaps I can influence its government through contacts with friends, if some of them might venture outside the city and meet with us." We skirted the walls of Florence, being careful to stay hidden in trees and brush.

Every time we passed a roadside inn or stopped to share our bread and *pecorino* sheep cheese with workers plowing and planting in fields, the talk was of Florence and Florentines. At each little village I listened to scraps of conversation about life and government in Florence. "You are my eyes and ears. Sit here in the kitchen and listen for me," Ser Dante would say.

A few of Ser Dante's friends, along with some of his colleagues among the White Guelphs, did manage to visit us discreetly just outside the city. These evenings spent with old friends were precious to my master. "I can almost imagine myself back in the *sestiere* of *San Piero Maggiore,"* he would say as he sipped his *chianti*, warming at every mention of a familiar place or event or person. I ate in the kitchen with the stable-boys, but my master treasured evenings at the tables in the *trattorie* with his Florentine friends, eating *tortelloni* with tomatoes, and reliving happier times. I was happy for him.

In each town—Pontassieve, Fiesole, Settignano—the news was not heartening. The edict banning my master from entering Florence was still in effect, as was the sentence of death should he do so. A return to his family and his prior civic life was impossible. We must continue to wander, and he would have to write in places other than Florence.

"Can Alessandro come with us too?" I asked.

"No, Benito. Fate does not allow you and me to be with family, but Alessandro's family is here and he needs to stay with them." My heart shrank, but I squeezed my shoulders together and turned up my chin. I could be as brave as Ser Dante.

Faced with the necessity of continuing his career in exile, my master decided to visit the neighboring city of Siena. He told me that he hoped to glean information there about Florence and Florentine politics. In the long poem he had begun to compose, the *Commedia,* he was writing about many Florentines, both his friends and his enemies. The Sienese could bring him up to date on people and events in Florence. Although Siena had often been at war with Florence, both cities had been renowned in the past for artistry and for good government.

On the last day Alessandro and I played in the Campaldino before Ser Dante and I left for Siena, I set up boundaries in the dirt and we pretended we were governors of neighboring towns. "My city does not want to fight with your city any more," I said. "Let's work together to construct buildings and to paint walls." We used bundles of reeds and twigs to build a central square, and we pretended we were elegant ambassadors, bending low toward each other as we approached from opposite sides. The field mice seemed to be laughing at us as they scampered underfoot.

Before we left for Siena I had more questions for Ser Dante about his writing. "What do you want your poem to say?" I asked. "I thought you were writing about worlds you make up. Remember when I told you if I were a poet I might invent *Natale* when it wasn't really the time of year for Christmas, so that I could be part of it whenever I wanted? Why do you write about real people in Florence?"

"Poetry isn't easy to explain. I write about what is real and also about what is imaginary. Sometimes happenings in the poem stand for bigger ideas in the world, or beyond the world. If those who read my poem recognize some real Florentines who have been evil, they may learn something about how to live and how not to live."

I thought about what he said. "Do you mean that if I write a poem about Beffa nipping at Galo, then people reading it will try to make their donkeys behave better?"

My master smiled. "You are getting the idea. Poetry takes us beyond the words. But it's not usually about nipping donkeys."

As he told me more about his long poem, I began to realize that among other goals, he wanted it to be a guidepost for Italians about how to be good people, just as Alessandro and I had tried to be when we pretended to be town governors instead of fighters. "To know how to be a good person," he said, "you have to learn about bad people too, so you won't keep making their mistakes." I thought about some mistakes I had made, like taking Galo out at night in Rome. "To write my poem," he continued, "I need to hear news of all sorts of Italians, historical or current, the bad as well as the good."

He told me that he was structuring his poem into three main sections: *Inferno* or hell, *Purgatorio* or purgatory, and *Paradiso* or heaven—three places where people's spirits might go after death. Those souls who were not sorry for what they had done were condemned to remain in hell forever, but those who were repentant could go to Purgatory to work their way out and up to heaven. He imagined a traveler, like other Italians but alive rather than dead, journeying through those places.

"Who is this special Italian who can visit a land where people go after their earthly lives, Master?"

"I have taken this role for myself. I am the poet and also the pilgrim. It is not an easy role."

"But no one has come back after death to tell us what it was like," I said.

"This is what a poet can imagine."

"Where do those go who have worked off the bad things they have done?"

"To heaven, to talk with the other blessed ones."

I thought about all this with wonder. My master was right that misbehaving donkeys would not be a good subject for a poem, if I wanted to write one. Perhaps instead, after I practiced my letters more, I would write an adventure poem about climbing down from a waterfall in the ice. Or maybe a poem about mending sides in a battle and becoming friends with those who had been enemies before. Then I thought about my master being the writer and the traveler both, in his poem. How could he do that?

"But Ser Dante, if you travel through a world after this real world, how do you get back to these hills and these paths and back to eating spaghetti again?"

He smiled the mysterious smile that always crossed his face when he spoke about his writing. "I can imagine myself alive even though I walk through a place where everyone else is dead," he said. "Then when I imagine I return and tell my experiences to those reading my poem, they will learn from what happened to me. Let me read you some lines I have written about that, where I am receiving advice."

Therefore for the good of the badly living world,
be careful
that you write down what you see after your return.

"Who is telling you this in your poem?" I asked.

"I have written about guides who help me," he said. "Here, the person speaking to me is called Beatrice. I knew a real woman named Beatrice once, when I was young in Florence. Do you remember my telling you about her, during our first journey south to Rome? At this point in my poem, when I have almost finished repenting for all the mistakes I have made, I say that Beatrice stands at the gateway to heaven. She is telling me what I must do."

I thought about our conversations, and I did remember. "You said she never spoke to you, and that she died when she was young." I said.

"Yes. But in my imagination she grew into something far greater than the girl I knew, something representing blessedness and goodness. She lives in my Paradise."

By now my head was growing heavy with all this thinking. Girls were to play with, to go fishing with, to swim with, but not to make into angels. "Ser Dante, your poetry fills my head with ideas I can't understand, and your *Inferno* sounds like a scary place. Can I think about it and talk with you more tomorrow? Right now I need to get Beffa and Gagliardo ready for the ride into Siena."

CHAPTER FIFTEEN

HEADING south and west from the hillsides surrounding Florence, sometimes we could see the tall curve of the handsome dome of its cathedral. Although it seemed near, we could never go to it, and as we moved on toward the west the great dome receded into the distance behind us. It seemed to be tempting us to come closer and then disappearing on purpose.

"Ser Dante, let's not make camp tonight. We don't need to sleep if we are so close to Siena. If we keep going we can be there by early morning. Besides, it will be fun to run Beffa and Gagliardo through the fields of flowers up ahead." I think my master was eager to get to Siena too, or maybe he was anxious to get away from the tantalizing outlines of Florence. He agreed.

As we neared the city and descended from the surrounding hills through grassy fields, spring wildflowers were just awakening, making the landscape colorful under our feet.

Close to Siena the flowery hillsides grew more orderly, giving way to rows of tilled land and tidy orchards. Continuing through cultivated fields edging the city walls, we walked though alleys of tall cypresses and at last under canopies of flowering almond and pear trees.

Ser Dante told me the world must be reawakening, and being a part of that new growth kindled hope in his own heart for new life ahead for the two of us. "In this blooming April," he said, "we may have new, warm corners in our hearts for the Sienese, even though they defeated us brutally in crushing battles long ago."

I was glad that he could feel hopeful even in exile. "Tell me about that," I said.

"At Montaperti, in the year 1260, ten thousand of my Florentine people lay dead after a bloody battle, and fifteen thousand more were taken prisoner by the Sienese. Worst of all, the Sienese captured our Florentine *carroccio,* the holy cart we always took with us in battle. My grandfather himself referred to the people of Siena as our worst enemies, and called the rise at Montaperti the 'hill of death.' Nonetheless, I can't believe that all the Sienese remain so hateful to us Florentines."

"1260 was many years ago." I tried to think about how many years but couldn't calculate exactly....forty, fifty years? "I would not hold a grudge against anyone for that long. If people are good at heart, they would forgive each other. Once at *Zia*

Bianca's, Iacopo took my bag of walnuts, my favorite ones that I used for practicing *bocce* ball."

"What did you do?"

"For the first two days I was furious at him and I put some pig fat on his favorite ball so it kept slipping out of his fingers when he tried to play catch. But then I missed being his friend so I cleaned his ball on my tunic, and he brought the walnuts back and said he was sorry." I was also thinking about playing with Alessandro at Campaldino, and how we changed from fighting to cooperating. It all seemed to fit together.

Ser Dante smiled at me. "You and Iacopo learned a good lesson. I hope the Sienese and the Florentines can be friends again too. If they can, maybe there might even be a chance that our exile could be lifted and we could eventually return to Florence." My heart agreed with him but my head was not sure.

Riding Beffa and Galo into the main piazza, dominated by the Palazzo Pubblico, we stopped to drink at the marble fountain. I knew that Ser Dante was eager to find some townspeople with whom he might speak about political news. Two dark haired Sienese boys—one slightly older than I and the other in his teens—were sitting nearby, talking about a large scroll unrolled on the cobblestones under their feet.

"*Ahi, ragazzo*, do you live nearby?" my master said to the older one. I looked at the younger boy, wondering if he might like to play dice with me, but I left the talking to Ser Dante. Instead, I hung close to Beffa's warm belly, putting my arm around his strong front leg.

"*Benvenuti*, welcome," the taller boy said to Ser Dante. "*Sì*, we live not far away, behind the cathedral. "*E voi*, and you?" He addressed my master in the polite form rather than the more common "*tu*," so he knew to be polite when speaking with grownups. Or perhaps the two boys were afraid of us. Our clothes were rough and dirty from hiking in the mountains, and no one would have thought Ser Dante was a cultured Florentine.

Nonetheless, they recognized his Florentine origin by his Tuscan accent with its soft 's.' "*Per piacere*, please, sit down and share our *pane*," the older boy said. "Although you must be traveling from Florence, you are welcome here in Siena. Our parents tell us that the *podestà*, the mayor here, has forgiven our old opponents and seeks peace. That is why he has asked all Sienese painters, even apprentices like my brother and me, to sketch designs for frescoes about ideal government. The best designs will become frescoes on the walls of the council rooms of the *Palazzo Pubblico*, under construction over there on the far side of the piazza. I am Pietro Lorenzetti, and this is my younger brother Ambrogio. Our painting masters are teaching us how to paint frescoes. They want every Sienese painter to work on designs celebrating peace, to display the *podestà's* message to the citizens of Siena. The new frescoes will tell everyone that our city is a model of good government, treating all the citizens fairly and well. Masons and carpenters are still preparing the walls, but in time painters will be selected. Everyone in our fresco workshop is excited."

Thinking about how people in Siena were working together lifted my spirits. I felt braver and spoke up. "*Buon giorno*, hello, Pietro and Ambrogio. *Mi chiamo Benito*, and this is my master." Ambrogio smiled and came over to pat Beffa with me.

Ser Dante brightened too, hearing that peace and civility were now goals of the Sienese. "Tell me how you will portray your wise government," he said with enthusiasm. "I may be able to help the citizens of Florence become wise and strong leaders. I am Dante Alighieri. . . ." But he stopped in mid-sentence when at the sound of his name the boys' faces clouded over.

"Ah Ser Dante, no," Pietro said, lowering his eyes. "Our parents have told us that you are banished forever from Florence. The Sienese *podestà* recently met with political delegates from Florence, and they still say they will kill you on sight, along with anyone traveling with you, if you dare return to Florence."

Dante sat quietly for a moment. "Well," he said slowly to the two Sienese boys, "if fate and God and the Florentine government have decreed that I shall always remain an exile, then I shall try to teach Italians as best I can, through my writing. And you Sienese will teach them too, with your frescoes."

I too had been thinking about good government, but the time seemed right to think about fun too. "Ser Dante, maybe Ambrogio would like to play with Beffa and me. We can be friends and I will share my bag of walnuts and my *dadi*." Ambrogio smiled and even Ser Dante managed a smile in agreement. Life had to go on even if we could never return to Florence. Before we began our games, however, Pietro told us more about their work as apprentices. I concentrated on what he was saying. Traveling with Ser Dante had made me a better listener than I had been up in the Casentino.

"Painting frescoes is hard work," said Pietro. "We must paint the design while the plaster is still wet, so the paint will sink in. It stays wet and fresh only for six or seven hours, so we can only paint a space that we can finish in one day. That space is called a *giornata*, since it is done in one *giorno*. I am older than my brother Ambrogio, so my *giornate* are bigger than his. He is practicing on very small areas first. We hope that the council members will choose us to decorate the *Palazzo Pubblico.* Then, people governing the city will look at the paintings on the wall and remember us, and in that way we can help shape a good future for our city."

Fresco painting began to sound intriguing to me. My master wanted to shape the future too. "Is painting like writing, then?" I asked Ambrogio. "But maybe more fun?"

"I don't know about writing," he replied. "But if you want to be a painter, it helps if you like to get muddy and wet, and it helps if you like challenges. Fresco painters must have good memories and steady hands, and work on high scaffoldings. We paint from the top of the wall down, so as not to drip on the *giornate* already completed. Sometimes my legs cramp from standing so long, and my arms ache from holding the brushes above my head."

"*Caspita*!" Ser Dante exclaimed. That was the word my *Zia* Bianca used when she commented on something amazing. "*Dio*! This task of making something beautiful to look at it sounds just as difficult as making poetry. Keep working hard," he said to the brothers, "I think that one day your paintings may teach the hearts of Sienese citizens. That is what my craft of poetry tries to do too."

Pietro and Ambrogio blushed shyly, looking at their feet. "We will try, Master Dante, but we don't know if we will succeed."

I poked Ambrogio's ribs. "You can do it, I know! I didn't think I could climb over icy mountains or stare down wolves, but with some practice I got to be good at it." Ser Dante looked at me with an expression I knew, one that meant for me not to brag about anything. I stopped talking and looked down at my feet too.

Ser Dante addressed the Lorenzetti brothers: "Benito and I bid you *arrivederci*. We must continue our travels, but we will return to see these frescoes of happy dancing citizens trumpeting peace and civility for the Sienese, and maybe for all Italians. My grandfather told me that his grandfather, *Cacciaguida*, said our city of Florence was healthier in the past than it is now, but I believe that Florence will return to its former goodness."

I thought about Ser Dante's grandfather and wished I had one too. As we walked back to the piazza where we had tethered Beffa and Gagliardo, I asked, "What did Cacciaguida say about Florence in the old days?" Ser Dante pulled out some poetry notes from his pack and read:

There were no bracelets then or coronets,
no women with gaudy skirts,
no houses empty of families

"My great-great-grandfather's Florence was then as Siena will be and Florence will be again: a peaceful and just place. Display won't matter, and people will love their families and treat their fellow citizens as trustworthy friends."

I didn't get to spend much time playing with Ambrogio, but I had learned that Ser Dante had found what he had come to Siena to seek: the news that Florence was still forbidden to us. We had made some new friends, but now it was time for us to head north again. It was spring, and warm weather beckoned us back toward the mountains. My master was glad that the good Sienese, like the good Florentines, wanted peaceful government for their city. He was glad, too, that there were others determined to create tributes to human goodness and hard work. A small voice at the back of my head kept asking why bad people kept eating into the plans made by good people, but I didn't think Ser Dante would want to talk about that right now. Part of my job was to keep him cheerful, and that meant not talking about sad circumstances. I swallowed my ideas and turned my face toward the mountains.

Once on the road, I jumped off Beffa's back and hopped from one foot to the other. "It is good to be back in the Tuscan hills," I said. As we went north from Siena, we smelled spring flowers as we looked out over the tidy fields. Ser Dante found the scene peaceful and eternal, reminding him of the circular repetitions of the constellations in the zodiac or the carvings of the labors of the months. He believed in good things coming after bad.

"It's no wonder that *Pasqua*, Easter, comes during April," I said. "The *prete*, priest, at *Zia* Bianca's church in the Casentino tells us Easter means coming back to life."

"Yes, the Christian calendar follows the seasons of our own Italian earth. This month of flowers sharpens my need to write. Since we can't find peace at home in Florence, I will create an inner peace in my poem for everyone who reads it. Sometimes the world treats us unfairly, so we have to struggle to reach our goals. My work is part of that struggle. The Scaligeri in Verona told me about their fortress, the Rocca Scaligera, on *Lago di Garda*. In springtime, with flowering lemon trees and lake breezes, it will suit our needs and will be a good place for writing."

Writing or no, the idea of visiting a lake in the spring sounded exciting. We mounted Beffa and Galo and rode north from Siena, back toward the mountains.

CHAPTER SIXTEEN

SINCE we had ventured so far south in Tuscany to Siena, we would have to double the distance we had come to return north to Lake Garda, beyond the Po River valley and west of Verona. By now, though, the Apennines in the distance ahead were our friends, no longer locked in snow and ice. On the way to the mountains, we passed through the gentle valleys north of Florence and Siena. This time we took a westward path, solidly avoiding Florence for safety, choosing instead a route through villages newly flowering with apricot and plum blossoms: Castelfiorentino, Empoli, and finally Pistoia, at the foot of the mountains.

"The path through Castelfiorentino is broad," I said. "Many travelers must have walked here."

"This town lies on a central route for Christians heading from northern Europe to Rome, the Via Francigena, so you are walking in the footsteps of thousands of pilgrims. Castelfiorentino means 'castle of flowers,' and it was here that peace was formally established between Siena and Florence after the battle at Montaperti in 1260."

It seemed strange to me that a place could be known both for Christian pilgrimages and for battles, but the town did look like a good place to sign a peace treaty. Its mud houses were decorated with cascades of pink and purple vines and its fields were yellow with sunflowers and daisies. From here northward the way was level, approaching the lazy western shores of the Arno River as it moved toward the Ligurian Sea. We walked on, reassured by a sense of calm and new beginnings. The springtime peacefulness also welcomed us in Pistoia, a town still nestled in the flatlands but backed by the misty outlines of the mountain range. The city walls were now crumbling from earlier battles, but between the cracks in the bricks and stones, spring flowers were pushing out their green buds and reaching for the sun. Now Pistoia presided peacefully over fields of flowers and crops, stretching south of the town where farmers worked daily trimming vineyards and planting vegetables. From there we made our way northward up into the mountains. Maybe Ser Dante is right that good eventually comes from bad, I thought.

As evening fell, I remembered looking at the stars when Ser Dante and I were at the monastery in Camaldoli. This time, he told me that if we kept the North Star always directly ahead of us we would be on track toward the marshlands and the Po Valley. We watched the position and phases of the moon for direction after dark, and during the day we followed the curve of the sun as it made its way from east to west.

When at last the valley appeared before us, hazy in morning sunlight and looking like a patchwork quilt of yellow and green squares of growing sunflowers and fruit trees, Ser Dante rejoiced. "From here on," he said, "we must avoid the larger communities, like Modena and Mantua, since I am never certain if people there will be friendly to us." Visions raced through my head about people trying to hurt us, like the knife-wielding madman in the goatherd's hut in the mountains. One could never be too careful, even in small towns or in the mountains. I tightened my grips on Beffa's reins.

In May, though, traveling in the countryside was a pleasure, and the *contadini* welcomed us, recognizing my master's polite demeanor and admiring his knowledge of farming. Sometimes we helped with spring planting in exchange for soup and bread and fruit. By now, up in the north, we were safely beyond the mountains and far away from Florentine battles.

From time to time we passed groups of well dressed horsemen armed with cross-bows, lances, and shields. Occasionally we saw ladies riding sidesaddle next to tiny pet dogs scampering along to keep up with the horses. "Ser Dante, look! These fancy people look like the guests at the court of the Scala family in Verona!" I pushed my chin down into my tunic, not wanting them to see what straggly travelers we must be, with our coarse brown clothing.

"May is the month for equestrian trips," Ser Dante said. "On the portal of the church of San Zeno, the May panel featured a horseback rider on a spring day." I remembered it. That rider was more warlike than those of the nobles we saw here, though. On the church door in Verona, the rider carried a shield and a lance, and was going out to battle. Either way, for battle or for pleasure, the coming of the month of May must mean the freedom to saddle one's horses and go out riding through the Italian hills. I plucked some yellow buttercups and stuck them behind Beffa's ear so we could pretend to be elegant horsemen. Beffa looked back at me with a lifted eyebrow, but went along with the game.

As Ser Dante, Beffa, Gagliardo and I rode along a rutted road lined with waist-high sunflowers, we heard a group of travelers approaching behind us. Some were on horseback, some on mules, and some walking. Dressed in bright colors and wearing wreaths on their heads, they shook tambourines and blew horns. Their enthusiasm was contagious, and even Beffa perked up his ears and his hooves. "Olà, Ser Dante, they must be celebrating May!"

Catching up to us, the revelers asked where we came from and where we were

going. We shared some wine, water, bread and cheese under a wide-branching oak tree at noon, and got acquainted. My guess was right. They were returning from a May celebration held every year in Assisi, far away to the southeast in Umbria. The festival was called *Calendimaggio* and took place for three days beginning on the first Thursday after the beginning of May.

"How old must one be to go to *Calendimaggio*?" I asked. "Could I have come?"

"You are young yet, lad," they replied, "but we will welcome you in a few years."

Their families had grown up in Assisi, and all the young people returned each year to take part in the singing contests between the residents of the upper town, called the Guelphs, and those of the lower town, called the Ghibellines.

Ser Dante winced at hearing these names, since the Florentine quarrels between the Guelphs and the Ghibellines had caused our exile. "But that is long past," the celebrants assured us. "We come together to dance, to sing, to make beautiful displays of flowers and torchlights, and to have contests in archery and flag-throwing. And mostly in singing! Listen to our contest song." I thought again of Ser Dante's belief that happiness follows unhappiness, and that evil can be overcome, and I smiled.

The music wafted over us. The descriptions of the contests reminded me of the *festa* we had joined at Poppi. "After the singing," one said, "we choose the most beautiful girl in Assisi to be Lady Springtime, and all the Umbrian girls deck themselves out in their finest dresses to vie for the honor. The winter can be long and harsh, and in May we welcome the return of spring in this celebration. Now we are on our way back home to our farmlands along the Po, to help in the fields. Walk along with us for a while." His muscled arm reached out toward us in welcome.

Ser Dante agreed that venturing out on horseback to celebrate springtime was far better than attacking enemies with crossbows and shields. Under the warm sun, with friendly villagers as companions, no one need think about wars. When we reached a small river, the Mincio, Ser Dante knew he was on the right track toward Lake Garda. The country people told us that the Mincio spilled out of the southern end of the lake and then continued southward, finally joining the Po south of Mantua and continuing eastward to the Adriatic Sea.

We followed the winding Mincio through leafy arbors along its banks and through some marshy flatlands, home to flocks of *gru*, handsome white cranes. I thought they looked like spindly white spiders, only with feathers. As they raised themselves gracefully on their slender wings, they crooned melancholy echoes as they followed one another through the moist air in long lines. Ser Dante jotted in his notebook:

And. . . cranes go chanting their lays,
making a long line of themselves in the air,
uttering laments.

At last we arrived at the shores of a glimmering lake, larger than any I had ever seen. The water was calm and blue, and the shoreline to the east smooth and welcoming. Far away to the north and west, I could see big mountain ranges rising and then dropping down steeply into the tranquil water.

"Ser Dante, those mountains in the distance must be taller than the Apennines!"

"Yes, Benito. Those are called the Alps, and they stretch northward to the lands where people speak a different language—*tedesco*, German."

Several small villages with white-painted low buildings were scattered along the lakeshore. The first, backed by an awe-inspiring fortress, bore a sign saying "Peschiera," or "place of the fishermen." The small harbor below the fort was crowded with small boats heaped with colored fishing nets. The local people told us they called the lake Benaco instead of Garda. The setting remained stamped in my master's memory, as he wrote in his papers:

In beautiful Italy, above the Tyrol,
at the foot of the Alps which enclose Germany,
lies a lake named Benaco.

A thousand brooks and more bathe the Apennino
from Garda to Val Canonica
whose waters come to rest in this lake.

Peschiera lies as a fair and powerful rampart.

There, all that the lap of Benaco
cannot hold must overflow
through green pastures and make a river,

When the water begins to flow,
it is no longer called Benaco, but Mincio.

CHAPTER SEVENTEEN

SER Dante scanned the horizon to the west, where a slim peninsula extended out into the lake. Crowning the sliver of land was a crenellated castle. Farther down the peninsula were the outlines of some ruins along the lakeshore. The tumble of stones there suggested a large villa, now fallen into disrepair.

"Benito, the Scaligeri counts in Verona told me they had a fortified castle on a peninsula at the southern end of Lake Garda. They also said that there were Roman ruins at the northern tip of the peninsula, so this must be the place. They called it Sirmione."

"Master, can I go out in the boats with the fishermen? We had no lakes near *Zia* Bianca's in the Casentino, and I have never been in a boat! I've learned how to catch fish with the nets my cousins and I made, but this would be real fishing."

"If they are careful boatmen and you don't go too far north in the lake, perhaps we can arrange it. It would be good for you to know how to take care of yourself on water. Let's find some good fishermen, while we inquire about the Scaligeris. The Scala family spends summers here, and they must count on dependable fishing families here in Peschiera."

We walked on the shore, sweet-smelling with blossoming lemon trees, toward the cluster of bright boats. Reaching a grassy area near the shoreline, we stopped near a small beach toward which several fishing boats were gliding. Two tanned fishermen jumped overboard, waded through the shallow water, and tethered the boat to a rock.

"*Olà*! What are you catching today?" Ser Dante said, explaining that we had lived at the court of the Scaligeri before, in Verona. "How do you learn the art of lake fishing?" he inquired.

"Our families have fished for generations. When we were young our fathers took us out on the lake, first close to shore and then farther up toward the German-speaking lands. First, though, our mothers taught us to be safe in the shallow water. We felt like fish ourselves, holding our breath and diving among the reeds. We look for *trota salmonata*, pink trout, and *carpione*, a species of carp. Both of them are delicacies native to this lake. May we ask your names, and why you are here?"

"My helper and I are traveling, since I can no longer return to my home. I am a writer, and the young Can Grande della Scala befriended us long ago in Verona. I am Dante Alighieri and this is my servant Benito."

"*Santo cielo*, heavens! We have heard of you. Some armed men came here last month from Florence looking for you. They cursed you and said you were circulating poetic verses with evil lies about rulers in Florence. They said there is a price on your head."

"They are cruel people," Ser Dante said, as his face darkened. "They burned houses and killed innocent people in Florence, and chased my family away to the hills. I have been wrongly accused."

The fishermen looked at each other. "They seemed like brigands, men we didn't want to trust," the first one said. "I remember that the Scaligeri counts said their castle in Verona had been graced with a visit from a great exiled poet, a man who had been unjustly exiled. Could that be you?"

"I am a poet, and I am in exile," Ser Dante replied.

"We can tell good people when we talk with them," the other fisherman replied. "Welcome to Peschiera."

I spoke up. "Is it exciting going out on the lake to fish?"

"Yes, if the weather is good and the fish are biting. Sometimes when the fog rolls in and the shore isn't visible, we feel like kings of the water, ruling everything we can see. If we have caught a good batch and still have some time, we can dive off the gunwales of the boat and swim. The water feels cool and slippery over your body when you dive in." I smiled at the thought, imagining myself in a misty wonderland. How I wanted to learn to swim!

In response to Ser Dante's questions about the Scaligeri family, the two young men told him what they knew of the della Scalas' presence at the lake. "Mastino della Scala, the *podestà* of Verona before the present Can Grande, built the castle at Peschiera, near the base of the peninsula," the first fisherman said. "Mastino was a great leader, appointed 'imperial vicar' of Verona. The great fortress that we call the Rocca Scaligera, out on the peninsula over there to the west, was built for him more than fifty years ago. Our own little fortress, the castle you see here in Peschiera, is a smaller copy of the imposing one there."

The fishermen told us that the Rocca Scaligera was used only for occasional hunting and fishing expeditions by the della Scalas. They lived in Verona still, but traveled to the lake to enjoy the cool breezes and the calm waters, and to explore the friendly countryside, especially during the summer months. The family had chosen the peninsula as the site for the castle because the narrow land jutting out into the lake was easily defensible in case of attack. The central part of the castle, a tall brick square edged by three towers, adjoined a fortified dock that was under construction so the Scaligeri ships could be moored safely. If any enemies ventured nearby and were captured, they could be detained in the dungeons at the base of the towers.

The lake also offered beauty, calm boating, and lemon and orange groves. The Scaligeri referred to their retreat as *"la perla di tutte le isole o le penisole,"* "the pearl of all the islands and the peninsulas." In summer the elegant Scala ladies rode out from Verona to enjoy the lake breeze and to bathe in the warm waters that came up from the bottom of the lake. I shuffled my feet. This talk of fancy ladies and beautiful summer retreats was all well and good, but when could I go into the lake myself, or out in a boat?

"Master, can I go with the fishermen the next time they go out on the lake?"

They answered before Ser Dante did. "*Certo*, you look like a strong young lad and can help us pull in our nets. How about this afternoon? Be back in an hour."

"*Bene*," Ser Dante said to me, "I will settle in to write, here in the serene beauty of Lake Garda, and you can learn to be a fisherman's helper." My skin tingled and my heart beat faster than before. I wished that Massimo and Antonio could be there with me instead of up in the Casentino with *Zia* Bianca....how lucky I was!

Ser Dante and I walked with Beffa and Gagliardo west to Sirmione, and I lodged the animals, eager to rush back to Peschiera to go fishing with my new friends. We arranged our few things quickly in our assigned quarters. It was May, so there was plenty of room in the fortress, before the hot summer season drew the Scala family from Verona to their lake hideaway. The castle guardsman offered Ser Dante a room with northeast windows overlooking the lake, along with comfortable bedding. Word had filtered there from Verona that he was a favored guest of the Scaligeri.

I said a hurried and excited goodbye to Ser Dante. "I have one question for you, Benito," he said as I passed the doorway. "You know how to swim, don't you?"

I guess he assumed that near *Zia* Bianca's my cousins and I had opportunities to swim, as his children had done in the cool pools of the Arno. He didn't realize that we had only creeks and shallow streams in the Casentino. For a moment I hesitated, because to say yes would be a lie. But what difference would it make? My new friends the fishermen would take care of me, and I would be safe in the boat. I could learn to swim later, during the weeks we planned to stay in Sirmione.

"*Credo di sì*, I think so, Ser Dante," I said. In my mind that wasn't so much of a lie as saying yes outright. I raced out the door and back to Peschiera.

"*Olà*, son!" they said as I ran up. We are twins, Giacomo and Guglielmo, but you can call us '*Doppio* G,' 'Double G,' for short. That is what our mother nicknamed us when we were small. We are going out looking for *trota salmonata*. You can help."

I pushed the stern of the boat away from the sandy bottom and jumped in. Some gray clouds were gathering in the east, toward the mountains, but I thought only of the thrill of fishing on the lake. *Doppio* G gave me a paddle and I stroked as the shoreline receded behind us.

When we reached the middle of the lake they showed me how to thread a fishing line with a piece of slippery bait and then sit very still watching for the *trota* to bite. You could see one coming up from the depths of the water because circles appeared on the surface, fanning out into smaller ripples. *Doppio* G pulled in two *trote* before I snagged one, just a small one but big enough to keep. "*Che spasso*!" I said, "What fun!" After half an hour we had caught a whole sack full of *trote*, and *Doppio* G showed me how to tie the sack to the prow of the boat.

I leaned back, enjoying the feel of the sun, until a cloud bank moved in. Sitting up straight, I tied my tunic tighter and looked out at swells forming in the gray water. The boat began to rock back and forth as a cool wind swept across the lake from the mountains. *Doppio* G told me to bring in the fishing lines and to sit very still, in the middle of the boat. Soon big waves were tossing the boat up and down so much that water poured over the bow.

"*Che Dio ci aiuti*!" cried *Doppio* G, speaking together as if they were one person, "May God help us!" I clung to the gunwales as the water came up to my ankles and then to my knees. "Turn the bow into the waves!" Guglielmo yelled, as Giacomo tried to maneuver the boat into the swell so we wouldn't be hit broadside. Suddenly a crashing wave hit the boat and I felt myself being propelled into the dark water. I sank under the surface, spluttering and reaching for the boat. The dark water filled my nose and mouth, and my arms and legs seemed frozen, unable to do anything.

At last I saw Guglielmo's hand reaching toward me, and I lunged for it. "*Dio*!" he cried, "I got him!" *Doppio* G wrapped me in their jerkins but I was still freezing, and the wind continued. "This spring storm blew in out of nowhere!" Giacomo called. I wished I had told Ser Dante the truth about not knowing how to swim. How could I face him? I wanted him to trust me, and I had let him down. My shivers were not only from being cold and wet but also from being ashamed.

Doppio G rowed as hard as they could, pointing the prow through the waves. After we returned to the dock in Peschiera, they took me back to the castle in Sirmione in their cart. I was very quiet, still chilled from the lake water, the winds, and the knowledge that I had not told the truth. The guardsman had a big fire roaring in the fireplace, and they set me down in front of it. *Doppio* G told Ser Dante how sorry they were for my accident, but that I had helped them nonetheless by catching fish and tying the sack to the prow so the fish weren't lost even in the storm. Then they told him they would teach me to swim, if we would be at the lake for a few weeks, so that I would be safe in the water the next time. My lips were blue and my teeth were shaking too much to talk, but even if I had been able to, I would have stuttered from embarrassment.

Ser Dante's eyes were stern and a line formed on his brow. "You could have drowned, Benito," he said, "but more important than that, you have not been honest with me. I would not have let you go fishing if I had known you could not swim. How can I trust you now to be truthful?"

I felt as big as the smallest *trota* we had caught. Ser Dante was right. I had wanted so much to go that I had not told the truth, and my lying had nearly cost me my life and had shattered Ser Dante's faith in me.

Finally a small voice inside me said, "Ser Dante, I am so very sorry. If knowing how sorry I am makes you feel any better, please know that I will do anything you ask to try to make up for what I have done." The voice sounded like an echo coming from somewhere else, not from inside me.

"It seems that your love of adventure gets you into trouble because it makes you act before you think sometimes, Benito. How can we sharpen your mind so you can control these impulses?"

The voice outside me moved closer and slipped back into my own throat as I thought. At last I said, "I have an idea, Ser Dante. I can learn to be a true helper to you, not only with the animals and in the mountains, but also with your writing. If you will teach me every day I promise to work hard, and then maybe I can help you, not with your poems but with the letters you write for your friends and your hosts." As an afterthought I dared to add, "If I succeed at learning to write, maybe you would let *Doppio* G teach me how to swim. I promise to work hard at both writing and swimming."

Ser Dante was stern but fair. He accepted my proposal and set up a schedule for me to practice writing on extra scraps of his paper, with some of his old quills. Within a week he set up another schedule, whenever *Doppio* G had a few free minutes from fishing, for them to teach me how to swim in the lake. I hoped I was growing up, now that I was eleven, and that my master could once again be proud of me.

Ser Dante's days established themselves into a pleasant routine. After rising early, he helped me learn my letters and then devoted most of the day to writing. He liked sitting by the window in his writing room in the Rocca Scaligera, hearing the lapping of the lake water and smelling the lemon blossoms while he wrote.

I treasured my visits with Guglielmo and Giacomo. When we weren't swimming we floated in the water, looking for smooth pebbles to use for games. I began to realize that if I relaxed and practiced, I could master the water. By the end of the month, Ser Dante let me write a letter for him thanking the della Scalas for their hospitality. My letters were lumpy and large, but Ser Dante could read them. I had learned a lesson, and vowed that my master could be proud of my truthfulness and my common sense. During this blossoming month of May, Lake Garda was a good stopping place for Ser Dante and me.

CHAPTER EIGHTEEN

THE lakeshore at the Rocca Scaligera in Sirmione proved to be a favorable place for Ser Dante's writing. His long poem the *Commedia* grew, and I helped him with his shorter letters. Diplomatic correspondence was a way for my master to help his patrons, in exchange for our room and board, and I was getting good practice at composing and writing too. The second summer brought sweltering heat, however, and many members of the Scala family moved west from Verona to enjoy the cool breezes. Lake Garda wasn't as peaceful as before.

Occasionally Ser Dante sent his own political letters to those in power in Florence, looking for justice and an eventual return. In response, his network of friends hinted to him that if he were willing to humble himself and admit his guilt, he could possibly return to his home and family.

"Of course I cannot do this. I am free from guilt, and pride and fairness will not allow me to return to Florence in such a subservient way. Justice cannot be compromised. We will continue our travels in exile."

I ached for him, since I knew that exile weighed on his shoulders. Word came to us that his brother Francesco was managing the family's struggling land and business affairs, and that his wife Gemma and his family were well, even though they were restricted to the farmland in the Casentino and were prevented from visiting us. The most recent Florentine traveler informed Ser Dante that his sentence of exile had been extended to the children, who would be tortured or killed if they ever set foot in Florence.

I felt as if a black spider were dangling over my head, ready to bite at any moment. In my master's papers he wrote:

There is no greater pain
than to recall a happy time in misery.

Reading those words made me think about the happy times I had spent in the Casentino with Ser Dante's children and with *Zia* Bianca. Those times would never come again. Ser Dante and I were trapped. I had thrown in my lot with him, and now both of us had to make the best of it. I told myself I would not cause any more problems for him as I had sometimes done. Extra worry was the last thing he needed. Instead, I would be as careful as I could and would help him as much as possible. After all, I was growing older and learning how to serve Ser Dante better, and we were partners in exile. A year had gone by, and in March I had passed my twelfth birthday. My legs were longer than any of my pants, and I could feel the muscles in my arms swelling a little.

New adventures always cheered me, so I was happy when my master told me we were soon leaving for Lucca. Travel in June would be delightful. Days would be long and food would be abundant. At San Zeno the portrait of June featured fruit gatherers and field reapers returning to their farms at the end of the day with baskets overflowing with ripe and delicious pickings. As we traveled, we were living examples of the monthly activities sculpted there. Thinking about that made me feel secure.

Ser Dante had received a request from a nobleman—the Marchese Malaspina—in the Lunigiana, north and west of Lucca, who wanted my master's diplomatic letter-writing skills. The Lunigiana was a forbidding region, less traveled than the mountain areas of the Casentino that we had crossed several times. But word had come to him that other exiles and other writers traveled and perhaps even lived there. He told me that even in the rough terrain of Italy's northwestern regions a strong communication existed, especially between fellow exiles.

"Remember the letter we received here from the poet Cino da Pistoia, Benito? He too was exiled for political reasons, and I have reason to believe he may be in the Lunigiana near Lucca. I would like to visit him in person."

"Does he write to you about politics, master?" I asked.

"No, Benito, he writes love poems. Do you remember my telling you we may be working for the Marchese Malaspina, near Lucca? Well, his name means 'evil thorn,' and Cino sent me a poem about a *malaspina* piercing his heart."

"Ser Dante, doesn't love make one happy, not sad?" I asked.

"Yes, if it is the kind of heavenly love Beatrice brings, as in my poem the *Commedia*. Cino is writing about earthly love rather than love in paradise, though. I, too, once wrote poems like that, but now I write about a greater love. If you think of my verses as a boat afloat in the waters of poetry, you will see that now I must write about more serious matters."

I tried to puzzle out earthly and heavenly love in my mind, but both seemed far away, and the idea of poetry as being like a boat was odd. Boats to me were for fishing, like that of *Doppio* G on Lake Garda. "How can a verse be like a boat?" I said. Ser Dante pulled out a sheet and read part of his poem to me:

now my ship
must hold a different course, being farther from the shore

"If Cino writes about the wrong kind of love, he won't reach his goal, Benito. If one writes about someone he loves on earth, he is bound by earthly rules. I want my poetry to soar beyond that, but sometimes it will be hard to understand."

I wrinkled my brow and thought. "Is the idea of the boat what you called a symbol?" I asked.

"You remember well. In the last part of my long poem, the part about heaven, I use the idea of a boat as just such a symbol, like this":

O you who, in a little boat,
desirous of listening, follow my bark
which, singing, sails on,

turn to see your shores again;
do not venture on the deep, for perhaps,
losing me, you would be lost.

"I like the idea of a singing boat, Ser Dante. If the boat that *Doppio* G and I sailed on Lake Garda had been singing, you could have heard it and sung back to it in return. Then we would have come back safely to shore and I might not have been tossed out. But, Ser Dante, what is a 'bark?' If it grows on trees, would the boat be made out of it?"

"No, Benito. Here, 'bark' comes from an old Italian word *barca*, which just means 'boat.' Poets like to say things in several ways."

I thought about this. "Do you mean that if I want to write a poem about the *trota salmonata*, but I don't want to tell people exactly what it is, I could call it *pesce rosa*, pink fish, and people reading the poem would have to figure out what I mean?"

He smiled and put his arm on my shoulder. "*Sì*, Benito. You are thinking like a poet."

"Maybe I could make my *pesce rosa* sing too, like your bark. I bet it would say to the other fish, '*olà*! Let's jump out and turn *salti mortali*, somersaults, back into the water.'" Seeing an expanse of flat green grass, I tried a few myself.

To get to the Lunigiana and then down to Lucca we first had to cross a rugged mountain range called the Garfagnana. If we navigated safely through those white crags, we could descend into Lucca. Ser Dante had learned from our friend Can Grande that the Scaligeris had strong allies among the Malaspina family. Lucca itself was ruled by a wise and brave man, Castruccio Castracani. The city had a proud heritage of freedom and prosperity, like the city the Lorenzetti brothers hoped to paint on the walls of the *Palazzo Pubblico* in Siena. Surely Lucca would welcome a great poet like my master, one with visions of justice and truth. If we could not return to Florence, we could count on other cities to champion Florentine values of fairness and beauty. Visiting Lucca would help my master shape his ideas about the best forms human society and human government should take. I wanted to meet Cino and the Marchese but mostly I wanted to explore the mountains in the Garfagnana.

The air in the mountains was cool and Beffa and Gagliardo loved it. Ser Dante told me to look every day for a creek or rivulet flowing south. When we found it, we would know we had crossed the mountain crest and were on the other side of the watershed, following the sunset toward the southwest. I looked hard, but at these high elevations I found it hard to search for creeks, especially in the early mornings and evenings, because fog banks often blanketed our path.

"Ser Dante, I cannot see my hand in front of my face! Do you think we will have to make camp here and look for a path tomorrow?"

He agreed and said that while we waited for the fog to lift he would write about it in his poem.

Reader, if ever in the mountains a mist
has caught you, through which your sight
was like a mole's, through a membrane,

And if you remember how, when the thick vapors
began to lighten, you could see faintly
from within them the sphere of the sun...

I wondered how a mole, tunneling underground, could ever find what he was looking for. At least Ser Dante and I and Beffa and Galo had good eyes.

CHAPTER NINETEEN

AS we found out in a hurry, the fog had also sheltered some evil people who had been tracking us. In the dark night in our campsite we were awakened by two rough soldiers wearing masks and heavy beards. "So this is the holy poet who has been writing filthy lies about the rulers in Florence. We will take care of you, *porchi cani*, dirty dogs!" The bigger one grabbed my master and bound his hands behind his back with a thick rope, while the other one lunged for me. His face was scarred, one eyelid drooping and the other crowning a bloodshot eye.

"Leave me alone!" I cried, jumping up and diving into the thick bushes behind our camp. The scar-faced soldier raced after me.

Ser Dante jerked his head toward me and shouted "Run! Run fast!" From my hiding place in the underbrush I saw the soldier looking for me. Ser Dante was right that running seemed best, but I didn't want to desert my master. What else could I do? They would find me sooner or later if I stayed near our camp. When the one-eyed soldier peered into the dark leaves in front of my face, I slipped between his thick legs and ran like a rabbit as fast as I could. I was fast, and he quickly gave up the chase. As I fled I could hear the first soldier telling Ser Dante, "Say your prayers and see if your god can help you now. And don't expect any help from your little friend. He will be running for days, until the wolves get him. When daylight comes we will tie you to your horse and take you back to Florence, where justice will be done and your head will float in blood in the Piazza della Signoria."

I ran far enough to be hidden in the thick fog that still blanketed our camp, and then I stopped and hid myself again. Fear gripped my heart, but I could still hear Beffa and Galo whinnying softly. By squinting I could see big dark shapes moving about in the clearing where we had camped, as the two men slapped Ser Dante hard and tied him to a tree trunk. Then they sat down, leaning against a rock outcropping, watching and keeping their swords pointed directly at him.

After a few hours the two captors closed their eyes, and my plan unfolded. I crept quietly back into the camp, soundlessly talking to Ser Dante with my eyes and my hands. His face and neck were bruised, but he jerked his head down toward the folds of his robe. I realized that was where I should look, and I found it! In a hidden loop of fabric was a small knife I never knew he had been carrying. Working swiftly, I cut his bonds, and we crawled toward the animals in the noiseless manner we had perfected in the Apennines. When we were a short distance away we could talk quietly, and I gave him a damp rag that I found in the saddlebags. He wrapped it around his neck and cheek, saying nothing about the welts rising there.

"Ser Dante," I whispered, "they have horses too. What shall we do?"

"Untie them, and we will lead them far down the mountain before letting them go."

Hardly daring to breathe, we mounted Beffa and Galo and headed west through the fog, leading the two attackers' horses. By dawn the fog had lifted, and we set the horses free on a path leading downward, far from the mountaintop camp.

"It will take them two days to find their mounts and they will never know where we have gone," Ser Dante said, "but we must remain vigilant." My heart seemed to be taking up all the room in my throat, so I couldn't even reply, but I kept my eyes wide open as we hurried down the rocky slopes.

Luck was with us. Far down a valley we saw a winding silver streak. Working our way toward it, we came to a small lip of level land near the creek bed with a fenced garden plot overflowing with beans and sunflowers, a small mud building with a rough tile roof, and a makeshift goatpen. No one was home; we waited. Finally, near dusk, a lone herdsman walked up the creek singing to himself as he corralled his goats toward the camp. He greeted us kindly. "*Ahi!*" he said. "Who are you? Summer visitors in these mountains do not come often."

"We are traveling to Lucca, and are godly people. Besides yourself, we have met only cruel Florentines chasing us," said my master as he introduced us. After our frightening encounter, he was testing our new acquaintance, trying to find out if the herdsman were genuinely friendly.

"I know nothing of your enemies, but your eyes and your words tell me that your hearts are good." My fear began to melt. The bearded fellow welcomed Ser Dante and me and helped me lead our animals to a trough filled with hay near a watering place in a curve of the clear creek. Then he put a pot on to boil. June was the harvesting season for beans, cabbage, and tomatoes. The herdsman cut up a handful of vegetables and added them to the pot along with savory spices and broth.

I smelled the steaming *zuppa*, remembering my *Zia* Bianca. "My *stomaco* is even happier to be here than I am," I said to the herdsman. He dipped a ladle into the pot and filled a rough gourd cup for me. Ser Dante quickly made friends with the mountain man.

"This little stream you see here," said the mountain man, is called the Serchio, and if you follow it down the mountain it will take you directly to Lucca, at the edge of the plains below. Perhaps I will accompany you, since I have not been to the city for many years, and I could use some parts for a new plow."

Hearing this news brought a glow to Ser Dante's face. The next morning the three of us, along with Beffa and Gagliardo, made our way along the creek bed south toward the foot of the mountains. The water zigzagged down the slopes, gradually leveling out as it reached the foothills above the plains. Here we rested, smelling the sweet summer air. I couldn't sit still very long and soon jumped up to gather wild apples from the trees and berries from the bushes crowding the hillsides.

"Look!" I called to Ser Dante and our new friend as the late afternoon moved into evening. "There are fireflies buzzing all around in the bushes!" Ser Dante smiled, and later wrote:

As a peasant who is resting on a slope
in the season when the sun that lights the world
keeps his face least hidden from us—

at the hour when gnats take the place of flies—
sees fireflies down below in the valley,
perhaps where he gathers grapes or plows...

The next morning we made our way into Lucca.

As we came near the city, the skyline above us was dominated by three tall *campanili,* each punctuated by row upon row of decorated arches and columns. From what my master had told me of Florence, I thought that Lucca must also be a city rich in architecture and sculpture, like Siena and Verona.

"I am gratified that we are returning to a civilized world busy with politics" Ser Dante remarked to me as we directed Beffa and Gagliardo up the ramps to the city gates.

"But I thought you were happy alone with your writing, at the Rocca Scaligera and in Camaldoli," I said.

"True, *è vero,* but I sometimes need the hum of the city too."

Our new herdsman friend, traveling to Lucca after years living alone in the Garfagnana, reacted with amazement to the city's buzz and sophistication. My master jotted down his reactions:

Not otherwise is the mountaineer confused
who, dazed, gazes speechless
when wild and rough he comes to the city.

CHAPTER TWENTY

LUCCA was a welcome change from our terrifying mountain encounter. Although Ser Dante had found neither Cino da Pistoia nor the Marchese Malaspina, we were glad to be out of the Garfagnana. We jostled into the busy narrow streets, and our mountain friend went on his way, searching out the tradesmen's quarters to hunt for the equipment he needed.

Ser Dante marveled at the ornate churches. Three in particular charmed him right away—those sporting the tall towers we had seen from below: San Frediano, San Michele, and the cathedral, San Martino. All were built in similar style, with horizontal rows of open arches and a seemingly endless variety of twisted and carved columns. Behind the churches we came to a curiously shaped open *piazza* unique in the crowded muddle of tiny streets.

"Look, master, this open space is like a long circle, instead of winding streets," I said. "Why would it be built like that?"

"Do you remember the Roman arena in Verona, Benito?" This area was once a Roman theater too, more than a thousand years ago. Look, you can still see parts of the steps and walls, some lying around in ruins and others now built into the buildings surrounding the *piazza*."

"Why did they tear it down, master?"

"The Romans were overthrown by barbarian tribes, and as the amphitheater fell into ruin it provided building materials for the three magnificent churches whose bell towers we saw from a distance. The marble stones left in the rubble found new homes in the facades of the beautiful churches in Lucca."

As I turned this idea over in my head, I liked it...using something old to build something new. Nothing would be lost forever, but just rearranged to fit new needs. "I used to be just a boy playing in the Casentino, and you remade me into a helper learning about the world with you," I said. "Maybe in a few more years I will become something entirely different once again. I might like to be an explorer or a horse trainer."

"You have not finished helping me yet with traveling and writing. But one day you will be grown up, and I think you will be a wise and caring citizen because of what you have learned. It would please me, too, if you would become a writer."

"Ser Dante, I have learned a lot about how to live, and I am having fun too," I said, thinking about my new friends and about learning to swim in Lake Garda and about racing Galo in the streets of Rome. Even if I had made mistakes, I had enjoyed myself. Or maybe *because* I had made mistakes I had truly learned how to enjoy myself.

We walked back to the cathedral, San Martino, where my mind turned somersaults thinking of all the things I might do when I was an adult like Ser Dante. The west façade was graced with beautiful carving. Perhaps I could be a sculptor one day. The most prominent statue was a life-sized one of Saint Martin on a horse, offering help to a poor beggar. The carver had captured the kindness of the saint toward the man. How amazing, that life could be recreated in stone!

We tied Gagliardo and Beffa outside. Inside the cathedral, beneath the lofty vaulted ceiling, I saw a frightening face, dark, long, and thin, with a mustache and a beard. Its body was stretched out on a cross, and the whole wooden carving was encircled in gold. The whole apparition seemed to hang in the gloomy air. "What is that, Master?" I said.

"It's the *Volto Santo,* Benito, the holy face."

"What is it? Why is it here?"

"The story is miraculous. According to tradition, this image of Christ was carved at the time of his death but was hidden for many centuries. People say that at last, maybe five hundred years ago, it was sent out toward Italy in an unmanned boat. It floated to the rugged coastline of the Lunigiana, west of here, where the bishop was told to put it into a cart pulled by two white oxen. Wherever the oxen stopped would be the permanent home of the statue. The oxen headed straight for Lucca, and the *Lucchesi* celebrate its arrival here every year in mid-September with a festival of lights, the *Luminaria di Santa Croce.*"

"What happens then?"

"The *Volto Santo* is adorned with a crown and jewels and is carried through the streets, accompanied by many torches."

I thought I would like the statue better in the torchlit parade than inside the dark cathedral, but the whole tale sounded made up to me. "Do you believe that story, Ser Dante?"

"Perhaps the story is not meant to be believed exactly, but rather to suggest faith or persistence, like symbols in poems." Ser Dante easily saw similarities between sculpture and poems, and now I began to see it too.

Sculpture fascinated him, and after he explored the carvings inside the cathedral

he returned to the west entrance to look again at the solid carvings of the twelve labors of the months on the façade.

"Benito, you remember the carvings at San Zeno. Look, here are similar ones about how we Italians live our lives as the months progress. The labors are like those of the country people we have seen on our travels through northern Italy." Beneath each carving was the name of the month in Latin.

"Ser Dante, I can read these names!" My master's reading and writing lessons had paid off. "Aren't the round images above the months the signs of the zodiac that you told me about at Camaldoli?" Ser Dante looked pleased. He must have hoped that I would learn more on our travels than just caring for Beffa and Gagliardo. He was glad, too, that I realized people everywhere busied themselves with similar activities in fields and towns, whether in Verona or in Lucca.

Ser Dante told me that Lucca's history was not so bloody as those of some other Tuscan cities, and from looking at the carvings he gathered that Castruccio Castracani ruled Lucca peacefully. "Lucca must be like the ideal city the Lorenzetti boys talked about in Siena," I said.

"Yes. In such a city, good government would be revered, fighting would be rare, and harmony would rule. People like us would not be exiled."

I noticed some differences in the carvings here, as I thought about them along with the ones we had seen at San Zeno. For December, the San Martino sculptor portrayed the actual butchering of the hogs, with their blood dripping into a bowl on the floor. In Verona the slaughter had already taken place, so the December scene there showed a return to other concerns, with workers gathering wood to heat their homes in the winter. For February, the Lucca sculptor featured fishing.

"In Verona it would be difficult to fish in February," Ser Dante said, "but here in Lucca we are further south and nearer to the sea, so it would be possible. We are looking at a miniature calendar of the work Italians do throughout the year. Every year each of us has a chance to rest, to begin work anew, to enjoy the fruits of our work, and then to return to rest."

"Ser Dante," I said, "before I came with you on our journeys I had not thought that art and poetry could be important…in fact, I had not thought about them at all! But now I see that they show us how we live. What would our lives be like without art and poetry to comfort us?"

"Art, whether it is in words or images, helps us understand the people around us and helps us learn to live better lives. Without art, life would be without purpose."

I began to agree with him, but my stomach was growling. "Our purpose right now might be to find an inn and a place to feed Beffa and Gagliardo, and a place to feed ourselves too. Aren't you hungry?"

My master smiled and unhitched the reins for Beffa and Gagliardo. Leaving the cathedral square, we walked toward an inn. Here, my master said, he planned to complete his diplomatic responsibilities and pick up his writing again. I hoped to make more new friends. Ser Dante's writing might last for his children and grandchildren and other readers far in the future, but I still needed to enjoy today.

June was a busy time for the *Lucchesi*. Both the San Zeno carver in Verona and the San Martino carver in Lucca were right about June's central activities. Some workers were cutting wheat with the circular scythe pictured on the façade of San Martino, and others were climbing trees to hunt for the ripest fruit to pluck, as at San Zeno. Even writing could not keep Ser Dante from delighting in the sunny June air enveloping the town of Lucca with its warm fragrance. Sunlight beckoned, and we moved from the inn, finding lodging just outside the city walls with a family who spent their time working a large vegetable garden. We both helped with weeding to earn our keep, and Ser Dante still had plenty of time to spend in his room with his pens and ink. We stayed at Lucca for some months, long enough for me to go to school and practice my reading and writing with the sons of the *contadini,* and to play tag and *bocce* with them after my studies.

We were not to stay at Lucca forever, however. News came of political stirrings in Siena, and Ser Dante was drawn south in search of news. If we had known of the disaster awaiting us there, we would have stayed longer in Lucca.

CHAPTER TWENTY-ONE

HEADING south we worked our way to the southeast, crossing the Arno River—its lazy curves much wider here, closer to the ocean than in Florence—and reentered the fruit orchards of Castelfiorentino. We had passed through here in May, when the apricot trees were overflowing with pink blossoms. Now, the boughs hung heavy with sunny globes—invitations to rest in the shade and savor the bursting sweetness.

We could not resist. Left untasted, Ser Dante said, the luscious fruit would soon pass beyond ripeness into beginning decay, faced with the relentless heat of the noonday sun. Such was nature's cycle, one that my master knew well, since his life and his travels mirrored it.

Past Castelfiorentino to the south, we reached a hilltop from which the distant dome of the Siena cathedral appeared to float in the wispy July clouds. Good and bad memories crowded each other in my head. It was in Siena that we had befriended the Lorenzetti brothers, but it was also there, many months earlier, that we had first heard of our sentence of exile in 1302.

"When we move into the city," Ser Dante said, "I will look for lodging for us at the *ospedale* of Santa Maria della Scala, where many pilgrims stay during their journeys from France to Rome. I may be able to find work there, too, in exchange for a quiet place to write. I have heard that the *spedalingo,* the officer in charge, may need some help with written correspondence."

"Isn't an *ospedale* a hospital?" I asked. "Can it be a hostelry too?"

"The *spedalingo* arranges care for the body as well as the soul," my master replied, "so Santa Maria della Scala provides rooms for Christian travelers as well as for the sick. They provide many good services, including giving food and alms to the poor, and caring for abandoned babies left anonymously through a turning box in the outside wall."

I thought about a mother and father leaving their new baby in a box in a wall. *Zia* Bianca and now Ser Dante took good care of me when I had no parents. Maybe the monks and nuns at Santa Maria della Scala were loving caretakers too. We stretched out under a tree on the hillside, giving Beffa and Galo a rest before making our way into Siena to find the *spedalingo*.

When I opened my eyes, I saw wisps of smoke curling up above Siena's skyline. "Master, why would there be open fires in Siena?"

Ser Dante awoke with a start, riveting his eyes toward the skyline. "Saddle the animals. We will ride closer to find out."

Reaching the next hill, we could see more and more smoke, and we heard wailing noises. A figure on horseback appeared from the northern gate of the city, racing toward us. As he drew nearer we could see his ragged and filthy cloak, blowing in the wind behind him. I realized that he could barely control his mount, since his right hand had only three fingers and his left arm ended in a stump.

"*Signori*!" he called as he pulled his horse to a stop. "Do not come any farther unless you want to die of sickness! Siena is filled with *pestilenza*!" His face and forearms were crimson, his hair matted, and his face sunken. "I too have the disease, but I still survive to warn others. Madmen are vomiting as they run through the town, and those who can no longer run are writhing on the streets. A holy fire is consuming my arms and legs, *ahi*! My brother swore he was being burned at the stake, before his hands and feet dropped off and he fell dead. I am fleeing because I hear that a pilgrimage to the shrine of Saint Anthony may be the only cure, *ahimè*! Families are dying and there is no one to nurse them or even to bury them. They are burning the furniture and clothing of those who have died, to try to save the few fortunate ones who are not ill."

Beffa and Galo pulled up short and turned their noses away from the stench of the rider. My heart filled with dread but I still leaned forward, taking in the horrific words and the maniacal vision.

My master maintained his composure. "Do you know the *spedalingo* of Santa Maria della Scala, near the cathedral?" he asked.

"Yes, he has not fallen ill and remains within the city walls attending to others who are sick."

"We must go to help him."

"But master, will we not become sick too?" I asked.

"That is a chance we must take, like crossing treacherous mountains in the winter," Ser Dante replied. "When friends and countrymen are in danger, we must do what we can."

The gaunt horseman looked at us in disbelief. "You must flee, to save your lives," he said as he turned to ride away. I heard the echo of his devilish laugh, unearthly and shrill, as he flew into the distance.

I felt my skin shiver and my heart jumped into my throat, but I tried to remain

calm so my master would not face this catastrophe alone.

As we galloped down the hill we could smell the acrid smoke, clouding our eyes and choking our mouths. The wailing and screaming grew louder, and we could hear pounding as if on a drum, and the sounds of wheels creaking. "Let's tie up Beffa and Gagliardo here, at an outlying farmhouse," Ser Dante said. "They do not need to suffer coming into the city with us, and we can come back to care for them later."

Leaving our packs with the animals, we continued on foot, tying parts of our loose belts around our faces to ward off the stench and the smoke. We reached the lower gate and began to climb up to the main square, dominated by the fountain where long ago we had met the Lorenzetti brothers.

An appalling sight met our eyes there. Carts with wooden wheels ferried dead bodies from the doorways of homes to a makeshift graveyard where workmen dug trenches. The *becchini* or gravediggers, dressed in black, their heads covered with hoods and their hands with gloves, were pulling off the bodies and stacking them in the trenches. Pigs and goats, usually confined in inner courtyards or gardens, wandered as well, looking for any stray scraps of food. Dirty children wandered the streets calling forlornly for "*Mamma*!" and "*Papà*!"

"Where is your mamma? Can I take you home?" I asked one tiny *ragazzino*. I could barely understand his words through his sobs, but I knew he was telling me his parents were dead or dying. "What about a *zia* or *zio*, an aunt or uncle? Or your brothers or sisters?" He only cried harder. I thought about how fortunate I was to have my *Zia* Bianca, even though I couldn't be with her. She would always care for me if I needed her. I took the boy's hand and kept him with me.

A few priests tried to conduct services for the dead, but the bodies were so many that only a few candles could be lit and a few drumbeats sounded. I shuddered as I saw several bodies lying in the streets, some without any clothing. Most of the dead had neither feet nor hands remaining, and the extremities of others were withered and gray. Those still alive ran through the streets tearing at their reddened arms and legs and shrieking "I'm burning! God is consuming me!" Others zigzagged hysterically through the streets, cackling like demons. In the corners of the piazza men were piling up chairs and bedclothes and curtains and setting them on fire.

Ser Dante accosted a man pulling a cart and asked directions to Santa Maria della Scala. "Take the western street up out of the piazza and then the first turn to the north, toward the cathedral. The *ospedale* is opposite the entrance to the church. *Per l'amor di Dio*, for God's sake, go quickly and then get out of here. We are all dying and you will die with us."

We found Santa Maria della Scala easily, because it was full of sick people and those trying to care for them. Some lay on blankets on the floor or on the street outside, and others roamed through the chapel and the anterooms screaming nonsensically and wildly waving their arms and legs. Ser Dante found the *spedalingo* quickly, recognizing him as he came out from the chapel carrying two large pots of broth and a stack of rags. There were dark circles under his eyes and he was thinner than anyone I had ever seen. Ser Dante introduced himself and offered help. "Dante! Why have you come? A famous poet is always welcome, but our city now is like your *Inferno*, your hell of which I have heard tell. Siena is grappling with a deadly *pestilenza,* Saint Anthony's Fire. Victims go berserk and suffer visions. Then their blood congeals so that it cannot reach their hands and feet and they feel they are being burned at the stake. I and my fellow monks are doing what we can to ease their pain and help those who survive."

My master took his arm and replied. "My servant and I have come because people must help one another in terrible times. We must work together."

Ser Dante administered scraps of food and water to the sick while I attended to those newly ill being brought by cart to the *ospedale.* I found a warm spot in the corner for the lost boy I still held by the hand, and brought him a crust of bread. Ser Dante and I worked without rest until nightfall, when finally our new friend told us, "Go now, to our abbey outside the city where you can rest and eat. My family lives next door, and they will welcome you. Come again tomorrow, but now you must rest. You will recognize the place. Turn to the west where a row of cypress trees goes off toward the sunset from the main road south from Lucca. Here, take slices of this bread with you. It is all we have remaining and is no longer fresh, but you need sustenance."

I nibbled at the coarse stale rye bread, putting the rest in my pocket to eat later. My legs could scarcely walk, but at least it was easier going downhill to the gate than it had been climbing up. Fortunately, the abbey was not far from where we had tethered Beffa and Gagliardo. A *libeccio*, wind from the southwest, helped clear the air so we could breathe without so much smoke. The *spedalingo*'s family welcomed us. They too had heard of the famous poet Dante Alighieri from Florence, the one who could never return to his beloved city under pain of execution.

Once we were settled I gobbled the rest of the stale bread. Then we both ate like starved beasts and I fell asleep almost immediately. Early the next morning Ser Dante awakened me for our trek back up into the city to help the sick, and read aloud some lines he had written during the night:

It has never shown so many plagues
or such bad ones, together with all of Ethiopia
and the land which lies above the Red Sea.

Amid this cruel and dismal swarm, I saw people running,
naked and terrified, without hope of hiding place.

CHAPTER TWENTY-TWO

WE stayed in the flatlands outside Siena for several more days. Each morning I climbed up into the city with Ser Dante, and we did what we could to help the sick, bury the dead, and cleanse the city. Some people recovered, and as soon as they were strong enough they helped us too, insofar as they could with mangled or missing hands or feet. When we went back down to the abbey at night, I helped the *spedalingo*'s family with the animals and the crops, and Ser Dante wrote until fatigue forced him to sleep.

On the third morning I felt hot and tired and Ser Dante told me to stay at home and not come to help. As the day wore on I felt waves of heat and cold, so that I shivered even under warm covers, and then would throw them off as if I were boiling. By the time Ser Dante returned, I must have been so feverish I could not talk, because he told me later he spoke to me but I said only incomprehensible things, and waved my arms crazily. When the *spedalingo*'s sister Anna and Ser Dante examined me they found the telltale signs of the disease—flaming redness on my arms and legs.

"*Dio mio*!" my master cried. "Our Benito has contracted the *ignis sacer*, the holy fire of Saint Anthony!" Sometimes I would awaken and think I was at home with *Zia* Bianca, and I would call out for her. I thought I felt her wrapping me in warm cloths and bringing me *zuppa*, and I thought I heard her weeping. Other times I thought I had died and was being tortured in the afterlife by horned devils with burning pitchforks, as my body stiffened with cramps and convulsions. "*Poverino*, the poor thing, he does not know us," Ser Dante said to Anna. "I will stay with him today, put cool damp cloths on his extremities, and pray for his recovery."

"I too will pray," Anna replied, "But we must do more. I have some holy water left here from a pilgrim traveling back from the shrine of Saint Anthony, and we can anoint him with a few drops. Also, in the sick wards of Santa Maria della Scala they use herbal ointments, like this one I have made from honeysuckle, nightshade, laurel, and pork fat. Spread it on his hands and feet."

They told me later that I waxed in and out of consciousness. All I can remember is dreaming that one moment I was in a sunny meadow, running through tall grass chasing butterflies, and the next moment I was falling, falling, falling. I rushed downward as if I had tumbled over the great waterfall, the Aquacheta. When I hit rocks at the bottom, I thought I could feel my body breaking up into little pieces, and then everything went black. Ser Dante told me later that I regained consciousness after two days.

"*Grazie a Dio*!" Anna said, "he is coming back to life." I saw Ser Dante kneel beside my bed and lower his head as he held my hand.

"Where have I been?" I asked. "Is it time to go up into town to help the people who are sick?"

"You are not going anywhere. You must put all your energy into resting and getting well. You have been very sick and almost died." I looked at my arms and legs, seeing the telltale withered grayness, and realized they spoke the truth. I stood up and my knees buckled under me. I fell back down, although I was grateful that I still had feet to stand on.

"Lie still," Anna said, "you are not cured yet, but I will help you get well if you rest." My head felt fuzzy but I nodded. I would do whatever Signora Anna asked.

The months of recovery in the valley of the Arbia River below Siena were pleasant. I gradually grew stronger, and was able to go out into the fields with Anna and her children. At first I just watched as they worked, and later I was able to help along with them as they harvested wheat. It was harvest time. In the south-facing fields, those planted earliest, workers were already threshing grain. Groups of three or four farmers gathered around the harvested wheat piled in rows by gleaners a few days earlier. Then, lifting the grain high in the air and pounding it with wooden clubs, they separated the seeds from the dry husks with rhythmic strokes. As the grain fell into baskets, the lighter chaff floated up and away in the breezes. Women and children—some even younger than I—collected the baskets, storing the grain till enough had accumulated to take to the mill to grind into flour.

In the north-facing fields, planted later when the sun was higher in the sky and the days longer, farmers bent over the ripe wheat, cutting the grain stalks with semicircular scythes. In a few days the threshers with their wooden sticks, followed by the basket collectors, would move to the newly cut fields and repeat the process. At the water-driven mills where the wheat grains were ground into flour, separate milling stones were used for grinding chestnuts. If the wheat harvest were small, chestnut flour could be added to the bread too.

"This chestnut bread is delicious!" I said to Anna and her family, "but I have to chew it twice as long because it is so thick and dense." As the harvest season lengthened, Signora Anna baked the chestnut flour into a hearty *castagnaccio* or cake that warmed the ribs of everyone in her Tuscan farm family. It was only then, months after I had fallen sick, that Anna asked me about the bread I had eaten. She had heard tales from her brother at Santa Maria della Scala that the monks now suspected that eating old moldy bread was making people sick. Of course all sickness—in body and in soul—might be traced back to questions of faith and belief, but poisons could arise from other sources too.

"*Ahimè*! When we left Santa Maria I was so hungry that I couldn't stop eating the pieces of stale rye bread they gave us," I said. "Ser Dante used restraint and waited till we arrived here at the abbey to refresh his stomach, but not me. Next time I will notice how the bread smells and I will wait for some delicious fresh *castagnaccio* like this."

Up in the city the disease had abated somewhat, but the *spedalingo* and the monks working at Santa Maria della Scala still needed help. Ser Dante resolved to stay near Siena throughout the winter and perhaps even through the next spring and summer, until those who had caught Saint Anthony's Fire could recover and care for themselves. Later, we would find a more permanent place to stay and he could concentrate on his writing. He told me that what we were doing helped shape ideas for his poetry. Although he himself had luckily not become ill—*grazie a Dio* that he had not tasted the moldy bread— he had lived through my illness and saw it as part of a miraculous cycle of rebirth. Working in the fields was part of that cycle too. We helped the farmers shepherd their crops from planting to harvesting to threshing, and finally to grinding at the mill. I had no choice but to remain and get completely well, and Ser Dante welcomed our longer stay. "Being here gives me a sense of belonging to the land and the cycles of the earth," he said. "Here, I feel rooted in the world." In the sunny fields below Siena, we could conquer both spiritual and earthly contamination.

The rest of the year progressed much as we knew it would. Before long it was once again harvest time, July and August. I had passed my thirteenth birthday several months earlier. By now we belonged to the farm surrounding the abbey, and the families of the countryside in the Arbia valley thought of us as true neighbors, honest hard workers like themselves. I had grown strong again and also much taller. "I hardly recognize you as the boy I took with me to Rome many seasons ago," Ser Dante said. I think I had grown wiser too. While I was recovering I had had time to practice my writing, and Ser Dante told me my letters now looked nearly as good as his own.

My favorite task was taking grain to the mill. I liked the never-ending background music of the rushing water turning the mill wheels, punctuated by the grinding noises of the millstones. Signora Anna sometimes let me bring along one or two of her younger children, who loved the mill trips too. "Can we picnic in the shade along the stream above the mill, Benito?" they would ask. After the picnics, they would play in the cool water, run after dragonflies, and poke sticks in the muddy creek bottom looking for frogs. Sometimes Ser Dante came with us too. He wrote about those lazy days in his poem:

a frog lies croaking
with just its muzzle out, in the season
when the peasant woman thinks of gleaning.

After the millwork was done, we lay on the stream bank watching the filtered light making patterns on the water moving over the mossy rocks. I felt at home here, knowing we were part of a larger pattern of life and growth that continued from year to year. Signora Anna's children depended on me for advice and for fun, much as I had depended on my cousins at *Zia* Bianca's. Being near death had taught me to treasure enjoying life in Italy.

The disease in the city was almost gone, and our time was freer. One day we rode Beffa and Galo to nearby San Gimignano to visit Ser Dante's old writer friend Folgore, who had escaped the illness.

"Good for you! I hear you are becoming a writer too," he said. "I write *sonetti*, sonnets."

I blushed, because the kind of writing I did for Ser Dante was correspondence, not poetry. "What are *sonetti*?" I asked.

"A special kind of short poem—not a very long one like the poem your master is writing. This group of sonnets I call the *Corona dei Mesi*, or Crown of the Months. Each poem tells about a month of the year. See, here is one called *Luglio*, July."

I smiled. "When Ser Dante and I lived in Verona we got to know well the carved sequence of months on the church of San Zeno," I said, "and we saw similar ones on the cathedral in Lucca. Artists and writers and country workers must all follow the same ideas."

Ser Folgore said that in his verse about July he wrote not only about harvesting and threshing, but about sitting in an *osteria* or café and enjoying the fruits of the season, sheltered from the sun and enjoying the richness of a *tavola fornita*. "What is that?" I asked.

"When the threshers have worked hard and are tired and hot, they can sit at a well-stocked table and eat chickens and goat meat cooked with garlic, and drink some good Tuscan wine. The feast is a well deserved reward." Ser Dante liked Folgore's poems, although in his own poetry he was working toward deeper truths.

"I, too, write about cycles," he said. "But in addition to those in nature I can see them in life and death and rebirth, as you have almost experienced yourself, Benito. Because you were so close to death I cling to life's joys even more tightly. All of us must do as much good as we can in the lives we have, so the world will be a better place after we die. In my poem those people who did evil deeds are punished in hell, those who repent can redeem themselves in purgatory, and those who work hard and are blessed will go to heaven. You and I and the monks at Santa Maria della Scala worked hard helping the unfortunate people of Siena when the terrible illness fell upon them. We work hard, too, at our writing to help those who will read what we write. As this harvest season ends, I want to move to a place of quiet and contemplation where I can fully devote myself to writing. You, Benito, can attend to our physical needs, and I will try to finish my long poem. Writing it will help the people of Italy too. All of us suffer, but we can emerge from suffering stronger than we were before. Our friend Folgore has promised to deliver copies of what I have written so far to people in many corners of Italy. His couriers tell him people ask for my work and read it greedily."

"Ser Dante, I am ready. When and where do we go?"

"There is a monastery at Sant'Antimo, near Castelnuovo dell'Abate to the south," he replied. "Tomorrow we will leave."

CHAPTER TWENTY-THREE

BEFORE heading south we rode north once again to San Gimignano, to deliver papers to Folgore, who had promised to help circulate Ser Dante's poems. Looping southward once again, we chose a road that wound back toward Siena, first through the Val d'Elsa and then along the Arbia. To either side of the river the Tuscan hills sloped up through fields of lavender and sunflowers, eventually merging with groves of fruit trees and melting into stands of scrub brush in the foothills. When the August sun beat down unmercifully at midday, we rested under cypresses along the banks. Early morning and early evening were the best times for traveling, when the pathways along the river were shaded and the sun's rays sliced through the leaves at an angle, splaying dappled light on the slow-moving river.

To the west, along the road to Siena, I saw high above me some towering walls, like a fortress, dominating the skyline. "What is that?" I asked.

"A fortified village called Monteriggioni, with high ramparts to deny entrance by anyone unfriendly. Count the towers."

"*Uno, due, tre*....there are fourteen!"

"It is a Ghibelline fortress, so we must stay out of view. Folgore says that the Ghibellines are still in power in Florence, and the Guelphs, our good compatriots there, are still hated. If the Ghibellines see us and catch us they will kill us."

We stayed in the shadows until we were safely past, but I still remember the imposing sight. Ser Dante remembered it too, because in his poem he compared the towers to giants looming over the lower regions of hell:

As, on the circle of its walls,
Monteriggioni is crowned with towers,
so, above the bank which surrounds the pit,

The horrible giants . . . towered above us.

To describe a Ghibelline fort as a part of hell must have given Ser Dante pleasure. If I were going to write a poem like his, I might put in my hell those mean men who came storming into our camp in the night fog in the mountains above Lucca. Poetry can bring justice.

Continuing through the Val d'Orcia toward Siena, we skirted this familiar city, where we had met the Lorenzetti brothers and where we had experienced the dreaded *pestilenza*. Stopping briefly in the valley below the city to say a final *grazie* to Signora Anna and her family near the abbey, we traveled southward, sighting always on Monte Amiata, a volcanic mountain dominating the distant view. Some of the path was familiar, covering a well traveled pilgrimage road, the Via Francigena, that we had followed on our northward journey from Siena to Sirmione many months earlier.

Passing through Buonconvento, on the third day we reached Montalcino, where my master knew he would find a friendly welcome. After climbing up through olive groves and vineyards to the town, we settled into an inn where the stewards brought out a plentiful meal of olives, bread, and cheese—the local *pecorino* made from sheep's milk— washed down with the local red wine made from the *sangiovese* grape. As in the carvings on the cathedral façades in Verona and Lucca picturing barrel making, Montalcino's inns were plentifully supplied with full wine casks. In the town *piazza*, coopers hammered new barrels for storing and aging wine. First they selected the best oak planks, those flexible enough to be curved into rounded contours. Shaping the cask this way allowed the winemakers to age the wine horizontally, bringing the grape seeds and skins to the bottom. Then they would remove the solid bits to clarify and purify the wine. Every year at *vendemmia*, grape harvest time, the barrels would be ready to start the cycle.

"*Com'e delizioso*," I remarked as I tasted the local offerings, remembering how I had reached greedily for dried peaches and a taste of Soave wine when Ser Dante and I first neared Verona. By now I had learned to be more polite, even if I was just as hungry.

The next morning we wandered a few hours in San Quirico d'Orcia, entering through imposing gates. The stone pavement under our feet was worn and sloping. Ser Dante said it was because many travelers had walked this way, taking the safe trading route to Rome by way of Lucca and the valleys of the Elsa, Arbia, and Orcia rivers. Going this way avoided the lands under the control of warlike eastern rulers, but there were still dangers of bandits along the roads and at the inns. All travelers had to be wary, and political exiles like Ser Dante and me had to take extra precautions.

"Why have you chosen Sant'Antimo for your long writing stay, Ser Dante?"

"It is far from Ghibelline territory, and the countryside there is rolling and rich. The monastery is particularly peaceful, and the Benedictine monks love music. There will be much for you to do in the orchards, olive groves, and vineyards surrounding the monastery, and I will have few interruptions. We will be happy there."

Crossing the river Starcia, we passed through a town called Castelnuovo dell'Abate and out into open country once again. There before us, in the plain below, was the abbey—a commanding structure of golden stone rising out of the feathery meadows. It stood alone, in the middle of a green field terraced with vineyards and surrounded by sloping woodlands. The building was of simple rectangular design, sporting a tall central nave roof flanked by two lower slanting aisle roofs, its rounded apse studded with three radiating chapels. To one side stood a handsome *campanile.* I liked the way the sun reflected on the narrow windows, as if it were inviting us to come inside. As at Camaldoli, various outbuildings surrounded the church itself—some for sleeping quarters, some for cooking and eating, and some for agricultural work. The sound of bells drew us closer.

"Ser Dante, something tells me I will like being here," I said. The late afternoon sun in August still blanketed the valley with dense heat, so entering the stone church was a welcome change from traveling. We tethered Beffa and Galo and set down our packs. Ser Dante knelt in the entryway, letting the cool luminous atmosphere of the abbey's interior wash over him. I felt I should whisper, as if we were truly in a house of God. "Ser Dante!" I said. "There is something amazing about the light in here!" The contours of the building dissolved in a golden haze suffusing the central nave. Afternoon sunlight streamed down from high narrow windows piercing the thick stone behind the altar, caressing delicate carvings above the capitals. I marveled at the intertwinings of humans and animals and monsters. "Are these *fiabe,* fairytales?"

"Some are," he whispered back. "Others are just pleasing designs, and some tell biblical stories." My eyes followed the rays of the light.

"Over there is a two-headed monster! And behind it is a strange beast with the body of a lion or a wolf, like the one we saw in the Apennines, except it has the wings of an eagle!"

"That is called a griffin," Ser Dante said. "A church like this includes all God's creations, real or imaginary. Some of the animals are like those in nature and some exist in the world of the sculptor, just as the fantastic creatures I invent live in my poetry."

I had more questions. "Behind the altar, why do those smaller chapels stick out from the main apse like little bubbles?"

"This is a pilgrimage church, and *pellegrini,* travelers going to and from Rome to pray, stop here and walk through the church, up one aisle and behind the altar and down the other aisle. The walkway is called an ambulatory. Other churches in this style line the pilgrimage routes traversing the holy roads from north to south. Perhaps some of the same pilgrims who stopped at Santa Maria della Scala traveled through here as well."

Above one column I found a capital picturing Daniel in the lions' den. "Look, Ser Dante. You can see the fierce lions and Daniel, and all of them are arranged in an upside-down triangle shape so that the capital can hold up the wall above. The carver not only has to include the characters in the story, but he also has to know how to hold up the roof!"

My eyes were glued to the capitals, not only because of the lively curling shapes, but because of a certain luminous glow that came from within the stone. "How can there be light inside the stone?"

"The light is not really inside, but reflected from the sunlight above. The capitals appear as they do because they are made of alabaster, a stone that is almost translucent."

"What is 'translucent'?"

"It means that light can come through, even though we cannot see shapes," he replied. "The effect is astonishing, isn't it? Sometimes light takes on a life of its own." He remembered it when he sat down to write:

I lifted my eyes and, as in the morning
the eastern part of the horizon
outshines that where the sun goes down,

so, as if rising from a valley to a mountain,
I saw with my eyes a part of the edge
dominating with its light all the rim.

Ser Dante's eyes moved over the building's stately interior, as he marveled at the power of this light. "Listen, Benito. Can you hear singing?"

I attuned my ears, realizing that music was gradually accompanying the light. "The monks are chanting," I said, "I can see them walking in toward the south entrance." After they filed into the sanctuary they took their places on either side of the altar, facing one another, and continued to sing, echoing one another. The beauty of the harmonies blended with the dense light. Ser Dante was transfixed, focusing both his eyes and his ears on this rich blending of light and sound. Like the light, the sound stayed with him, as he wrote in his poem about Heaven:

And from within those who appeared in front
"Hosanna" sounded so sweetly that never since
have I been without desire to hear it again.

Both of us stood still, mesmerized by the sound and light enveloping us. As the chant came to a close, a young Benedictine only slightly older than I approached us, introducing himself. "*Benvenuti*, honored guests, welcome. I am Teódoro, an apprentice monk. How may I serve you?"

Dante thanked Teódoro, asking for further explanation about the chanted music. Teódoro explained that the chant was not music in the usual sense, because no one played a musical instrument. Instead, as part of their vows of poverty, chastity, and obedience, the monks chanted the simple notes in Latin. *Canto Gregoriano* or Gregorian chant had been named after Pope Gregory, he said. In Sant'Antimo its pure notes resonated with the perfect acoustics in the marble church, reflecting simplicity and holiness.

Teódoro smiled at me and I knew right away that we would become friends. "I am learning to be a monk," he said, "but I still live in the nearby town with my family. You can call me Teó if you like. Would you like to tour the monastery? Later I can take you to visit my home. Word of your arrival has come before you. You must be the servant of the famous poet Dante, who is seeking peace and salvation through his writing." I felt as if some of Ser Dante's fame had rubbed off on me. People had heard of me, so far away from my home with *Zia* Bianca in the Casentino.

The kitchens must have been as busy as beehives because tempting odors were wafting all around us, even in the sanctuary. Several of the monks who had been chanting now returned to the church to scrub the walls and the floor. I asked Teó if this cooking and cleaning happened every day.

"No, today is a special day. Tomorrow is *ferragosto*, August fifteenth, the *Festa dell' Assunta*, or Feast of the Assumption of Mary!" Teó exclaimed. "On that day Italians celebrate the joyful departure of the mother of Jesus as she ascends into the heavens. The *festa* is also a time for all of us living in these river valleys to give thanks for our harvest and for our good health. Come, I will find rooms in the monastery for your stay, and then you can celebrate with my family in Castelnuovo dell'Abate."

Teó's family was boisterous. He had two older sisters and two younger brothers, and the boys ran to me at once. "Come!" they said, "we have built a tree house behind our cottage, and we can eat our *torta* and our apples there."

I felt as if I were home again, with *Zia* Bianca and my cousins, or with Signora Anna and her children near Siena. Teó asked his mother if I might stay with them while Ser Dante lived at the monastery close by. I could visit there every day, care for Beffa and Gagliardo, work with Teó as he learned how to be a monk, and see what work needed to be done, both at the monastery and at the cottage. Perhaps I would even learn to chant! Ser Dante would have time to write, and I would gain a new family.

Ser Dante and I remained with the Benedictine monks at Sant'Antimo for two years. I learned how to cultivate and harvest the fruits and vegetables of the Starcia River valley, and I memorized the Latin phrases and simple melodic lines of Gregorian chant. Teó's mother told me I had a most pleasing voice and that I should consider becoming a monk. The idea was tempting, but I was committed to helping Ser Dante, and I knew he would move on after he had completed the bulk of his poem. Besides, I loved the gaiety of life in the countryside. Living seemed especially sweet to me after my bout with disease near Siena.

One loss remained, though....an empty place in my heart for my *Zia* Bianca and my cousins. Would I ever see them again? New friends filled my life, but nothing could fully replace my home and my family. Sometimes when Ser Dante and I walked through the olive groves in the evening, we would talk about our lives as they once were, before the turmoil of rebellion and exile. My master never complained, but I could tell that the enforced separation from Gemma, the children, his brother, and his half-brother and half-sisters gnawed at him too.

"Gemma always eased my life," he would say. "Due to her caring attention, our children must now be going forth into the world as compassionate citizens. When couriers take my poetry back to Florence, I tell them first to deliver my personal affection and thanks to her. How I love to imagine what Giovanni and Pietro and Iacopo and Antonia talk about, sitting gathered at our table in the evening after a busy day."

Putting this ache in the bottom of his heart, Ser Dante was happy at Sant'Antimo, and I learned to live for our daily lives there too, instead of trying to live in the past. The daily routine of the Benedictines reminded us of our stay at Camaldoli. The lives of the monks parallelled Ser Dante's own, dedicated to *ora et labora*, prayer and work. The regularity of the *campane*, bells, echoed the diligence of the monks as they painstakingly copied manuscripts. Ser Dante and the monks shared a love of books, which were scarce and valuable. He hoped that the book he was writing—his long poem the *Commedia*, evoking God and tracing the pathway of humans toward understanding themselves and understanding their places in God's universe—would become a treasure for readers too. The cool travertine marble of the abbey of Sant'Antimo, permeated with warm golden light filtered through the alabaster carvings, provided him a tranquil place for contemplation. It was a comforting and welcoming place for me too. I began to imagine what life might hold for me in the future.

CHAPTER TWENTY-FOUR

LEAVING Sant'Antimo and my new friend Teó and his family was bittersweet for me. I had grown in many ways during my stay at the abbey. I had nearly died from Saint Anthony's Fire and my body and spirit were weak. When Ser Dante and I first came to the abbey, at night when I awoke I would think that I was dead and wandering with him in the afterlife he wrote about. I thought I could feel cold winds and hear menacing noises, and I would wake up perspiring only to realize I was alive and safe.

I had needed a quiet place to rebuild my strength, and the stay with the monks and with Teó and his family had been ideal. I had learned to sing, I had improved my writing, and I had become so capable about work in the fields that the Benedictines had designated me as *capo* or chief among my group of planters and harvesters. I had grown happy again, and I had grown taller, above Ser Dante's shoulder! Teó's family had become almost like my *Zia* Bianca and my cousins. But Ser Dante was by now my true family, a father to me, and I would follow him anywhere. Now that I knew how to write, I could send Teó letters so we would remain close even after I left. Ser Dante spoke to me about his plans.

"Now that I am working on the last segments of the poem, I need to move back to cities, to talk with other writers and with government officials. If we choose our locations carefully, we will be safe. The letters the monks have brought to me say that several cities in the north, including Parma and Padua, are under Guelph control and that we would be welcomed there. The nearby republic of Venice is safe too, because it has its own independent government. Their rulers have never bowed to the cruelties of the Ghibellines. Folgore and Cino da Pistoia and my other correspondents tell me that I am becoming famous, and that copies of parts of my poem are circulating. They say that rulers are eager for me to visit their courts, to read my poem aloud and to talk with learned people."

"They speak also of other accomplishments in painting and in sculpture, works I have heard about but have never seen. You and I have experienced much—seeing fresco painting about good government in Siena, studying church carvings in Verona and in Lucca, learning about Gregorian music and monastery life in Camaldoli and Sant'Antimo, and fighting the terrible illnesses that have felled many of our countrymen. But there is always more to learn. I want to see for myself some of the great creations, like the sculpture of Antelami in the Baptistery in Parma. In Padua, my Florentine friend Giotto is painting astounding frescoes. I try to create realistic portrayals in my poems, and both these artists do this too, in stone or in paint. We share goals."

As he spoke I thought about his lofty goals. What could I do, one day, to make the world more beautiful and wiser, as he was doing?

He continued: "The Guelph leaders in Parma and Padua may even make it possible for us to reconnect with friends and family from Florence. Some of the letters I have received hint that some day my wife Gemma and my children may join us without fear of reprisal."

"And my cousins, and *Zia* Bianca? It will be wonderful to see Giovanni, Pietro, Iacopo, and Antonia!" I said.

"*Speriamo*, we will hope. Most importantly, I have new work for you. Beffa and Gagliardo and I still need you to make living and traveling easier, but the new responsibilities will use your sharp mind too. I have noticed how thoughtful and polite you have become, and how quickly you learn. You shape your letters neatly, and use our melodious Italian language well. I want you to be my secretary as well as my servant. You can write letters that I dictate, and then go off by yourself—with Gagliardo—to deliver them as I request."

I stood up straighter and looked Ser Dante in the eye. "*Grazie*. I am honored. I can take care of myself on trips such as you suggest, and I am pleased to be a part of your great work." He was giving me a chance to prove myself as an adult. We said *arrivederci* to our good friends in Sant'Antimo and prepared for the trip north.

Cheese and ham were the crowning glories of early fall in the region around Parma, where we were headed. Pigs were plentiful, and in the autumn farmers would slaughter the fattened hogs to make thin delicious Parma ham, *prosciutto*. Fall was a time for feasting and rejoicing. The *vendemmia*, or grape harvest time, brought forth a sense of work well done. All the care, time, and energy put into early planting, pruning, and shepherding now bore fruit, and workers could begin to unwind. Herdsmen in the foothills of the Apennines watched the goats and the sheep, now fat creatures stretched out contentedly in the hazy September sun. Ser Dante wrote in his papers:

As goats, agile and wanton on the heights
before they have eaten, become tame

when ruminating, lying silent and quiet

In the shade while the sun is hot,
watched over by the herdsman who leans
on his staff, and while leaning guards them;

. . . . the shepherd who lodges in the open
passes the night beside his flock,
watching lest a wild beast scatter it.

Descending from the green slopes, we stopped to gaze over the rich flat country spreading north. Abundant farmlands and vineyards extended as far as we could see.

"Who is this Antelami of whom you spoke?" I asked.

"His name was Benedetto Antelami and he was a skilled artist, working nearly a hundred years ago. You will see his lifelike carvings when we reach the center of Parma."

Soon we saw a bell tower piercing the sky in the distance, and next to it an imposing shape. "That is the *duomo* or Cathedral of Parma, Santa Maria Assunta," Ser Dante said. On the tall building, I could barely make out a series of lacy colonnaded arches.

Winding through the narrow lanes closest to the center of the city, we emerged into an open area just as the brightest sunlight broke from the clouds to highlight the west facade of the cathedral. Ser Dante stopped, breathless. I caught my breath too. The building was magnificent.

"Is this the Baptistery? So this would be the place where babies are baptized, like the Baptistery of San Giovanni you told me about in Florence?"

"Yes. I have wanted to see its interior ever since we saw the carvings of the labors of the months in Verona. Everyone says that Antelami's own cycle of the monthly labors is larger, more robust, and more detailed than any earlier ones. Let's go in."

I tugged at the towering ancient door, creaking on its hinges. As always, Ser Dante used every experience in his writing, so he noted when describing the gate of Purgatory:

And . . . the pivots of the sacred door
which are of metal, resonant and strong,
began to turn on their hinges.

Once we were inside, the darkness dissipated and filtered light from the lofty windows illuminated the art below. The coolness and quiet surrounded us. Ser Dante focused first on the baptismal font, which was octagonal, like the building itself. It was carved from one gigantic piece of pink marble, the kind found in Verona. "The builders must have brought it from Verona to Parma by canal," he said. I tried to imagine this but it seemed impossible. How could even a group of strong men lift such a thing?

Turning our eyes upward toward the dome, we saw the figures of the months. They were accompanied by the signs of the zodiac, because—as we had often seen—the movement of the stars and that of the seasons paralleled one another. I had only recently learned about stone carving, but I could see that these were masterful. "This Antelami knew how to show strong muscles and how to show folds in clothing, to make these laborers just like real working Italians! They look as if they could walk out of the stone to greet us."

Antelami had executed the sculptures almost in the round, so that they stood out from the stone background like living workmen. The sculptures were simple but powerful evocations of the *rituale campestre* or cyclical monthly work in the countryside. Although they were nearly a hundred years old, a century did not seem long in the wider scope of human life that fascinated Ser Dante.

"Do you know, Benito, I can sense Antelami's spirit still hovering here, shaping a head here and polishing a hand there." Ser Dante stood wide-eyed, absorbing the carvings as he walked slowly around the Baptistery's interior, gazing up at the sculptures just below the dome.

The December figure, cutting firewood for winter warming, was particularly robust and muscular. His arm, holding a scythe, was carved as a separate bridge of stone, not connected to the back panel of the relief sculpture. "How can a sculptor do this?" I said. "If I tried, I'm sure the stone would break." The same depth shone forth from September's grape harvester, whose knife appeared to cut through freestanding thick grapevines detached from the stone background.

"Look, touching the harvester's foot is the zodiac figure of Libra, holding her balance scales."

"Tell me about Libra, Ser Dante."

"She represents balance, harmony, and cooperation between people. That is why you see her with scales, weighing matters carefully. Or, literally, she means a balance between the *vendemmia* going on in the fields outside and the September *vendemmia* carved here in the Baptistery. There is a powerful kinship here between nature and art, as well as a sense of human authority."

"Look. There are two extra carved figures here, at either end of the cycle of the twelve months. Who is this old man with a scroll, and who is the young woman?"

"I think they represent winter and spring, larger seasons of the year. Everything fits into its proper place. One goal I have in my poetry is to show the position and destiny of human beings in the world as they work through cycles of natural blessings, and that must have been one of Antelami's goals too."

Toward the north doorway of the Baptistery Ser Dante noticed a carved signature there of the sculptor himself: Benedetto Antelami. He told me that most medieval sculptors worked anonymously, for the glory of God rather than for their own glory. But this proud sculptor had written his name by his work, so that visitors to the Baptistery for years to come would remember him. Ser Dante smiled in recognition. He, like Antelami, was proud of his own work.

"Early in my poem," he said, "I have envisioned a special place for myself, among the great poets of the past, from Greece and Rome, who occupy a pleasant green oasis at the edge of the underworld. I write of visiting them there":

Thus I saw assembled the school
of that lord of the lofty song.

After they had talked together a little
they turned to me with signs of greeting,

And still more honor they showed me
by making me one of their group,
so that I was the sixth among such sages.

"Is it not boastful to think one's own work great?" I asked.

"If you believe in yourself, you must have faith in your own ability to move others with your art. But let us go on to other skills. I commission you to travel north to Verona to take a letter to our old friend, Can Francesco della Scala. He can help me distribute my work. You will leave tomorrow."

"*Certo*," I said, squeezing the muscles of my face together so as not to show my excitement. My first trip alone!

CHAPTER TWENTY-FIVE

BEFFA was sad when I left him in the stable, so I gave his muzzle a soft stroke while I fitted Gagliardo with a bridle. I had never taken Gagliardo out by myself. I packed a few provisions in the saddlebag and started out, keeping the letter for Can Grande in a safe place inside my shirt. Ser Dante told me that Can Grande now ruled in place of his brother Alboino, whose weak leadership had endangered Verona. First I rode across the plains to the Po River, making camp for the night near Mantua. From there I knew the way, because I would follow the Mincio, the tributary of Lake Garda where Ser Dante and I had been before.

The next morning Gagliardo and I waded north through the reedy marshes along the Mincio. I watched the egrets standing like princes in the shallow water and the cranes flying gracefully overhead, and I thought about how much fun it would be to be a bird and fly wherever I wanted. I felt free, going off by myself to deliver Ser Dante's letter. In the heat of the afternoon I stopped under an olive tree to give Gagliardo a rest. Nearby was a fishermen's shed of rushes and grass, and I lay down inside it and closed my eyes.

I awoke with a start, hearing rude voices shouting "*Porca miseria*! Hell! *Che flebo*, What a weakling! We can take him with no trouble at all. He will eat dust before we are through with him."

Standing over me were two rough men, dressed in torn dirty tunics and sporting scraggly beards. I could see the knives in their belts, and the clubs slung across their backs. "Hand over your money, *ragazzino*. And give us all you have to eat, too. And don't go crying for your *mamma*. Nobody can hear us." They had untied Gagliardo, who pranced nervously, and one of them was busy attaching my horse's reins to a rope behind his own steed.

"I am not a *ragazzino*, and I know how to fight," I said. "Give me back my horse. My friends are nearby and will return in a moment."

"You have no friends and nobody is anywhere near here, liar. Give us everything in your pack."

"I have no money and very little to eat. Here, take a look." I handed them my pack, trying to look as brave as I could but wishing Ser Dante were with me to help.

"You are joking. Someone must have sent you on a mission, so you must be carrying some *soldi*." They looked through my belongings and found I was telling the truth. I carried almost nothing. The taller one punched me in the jaw and pushed me back onto the grass, saying, "Well, we can take your horse at least." I watched them mount their horses and gallop away, pulling my pawing horse behind them. As Galo turned back to look at me I saw pleading and fear in his eyes.

What would Ser Dante think? On my very first task alone I had let him down, and his trusted horse Gagliardo was gone. What could I do? The years of travel with Ser Dante had strengthened my courage and taught me how to get myself out of tough situations. I knew if I walked north, following the Mincio, I would eventually reach Peschiera. There, I could look for my friends *Doppio G*, and they would help me get to Verona to deliver Ser Dante's letter to Can Grande. But first I had to rescue Galo! Since there might be other *briganti* nearby, I hid in the shade for a few minutes and then started off after them.

Within an hour I spotted them up ahead, sprawled under a tree by the river while they guzzled wine and stuffed food into their already bulging bellies. Their horses were tied to another tree farther from the shore, along with Galo, still nervously arching his neck and pawing the ground. I waited in a rocky hollow till the food, the wine, and the hot sun caused their eyes to close and their heads to loll on their shoulders, and then I made my move. Picking up several large stones, I threw one after another into the eddy of the Mincio directly in front of the sleeping men. While I threw them I yelled, in a rude and muscular voice, crude threats. "*Che schifo*! How revolting! These lazy robber bums can't even keep their eyes open to guard their loot. We'll show them what REAL thieves can do!"

Every time I yelled I changed my voice, to give the impression of a horde of villains charging in. Armed with more rocks, I kept throwing, now directly toward the tree and the snoring men. They rolled over and their foreheads collided as they drunkenly stumbled up to defend themselves. Lurching to their feet, they crashed into each other once more, their fat bellies bouncing down the slope toward the river. As I heard the giant splash I turned back to see them flailing wildly about in the water, and then I made a dash for Galo's tree.

"*Bene*, my friend. I'm back. We're getting out of here," I whispered in his ear as I untied him as fast as I could, leaping onto his back and digging my heels into his flanks. He shot off like lightning and we raced all the way to Peschiera, hardly ever looking back. We were both exhausted and hungry by the time we reached the fishing town, but exhilarated at having outwitted the *briganti*.

I found *Doppio G* just returning from fishing, and they hugged me with delight. "But where is Ser Dante? Where is Beffa? Are you coming to stay at the Rocca Scaligera again?" I told them of my escape and they clapped me on the shoulders. "*Complimenti*! Ser Dante will be proud of you! Stay with us tonight, and after a good night's sleep and some *pasta*, we'll send you on your way to Verona."

I thanked them but said I would prefer to take some bread and dried fish with me and get to Verona right away. After resting Galo a short while, I saddled him again and rode directly to the Scaligeri castle. Can Grande and I hardly recognized each other. He, like me, had grown much taller. Now he was truly a young lord, regal and proud. I told him of my encounter with the thieves along the Mincio, describing where they were, what they looked like, and what kinds of horses they had. "I will send my *cavalieri*, my palace guards, after them right away," he said, "arresting these good-for-nothings and putting them in our prison will teach them a lesson and make the territory of Verona safer."

I told him about my new responsibility as courier for Ser Dante, and his face brightened.

"Your master Dante helped my family greatly. How goes it with him?" I pulled out the letter—*grazie a Dio* that I had held it tight to my chest inside my shirt, when the thieves accosted me—and bowed low as I handed it to Can Grande. He read aloud: "To the great and most victorious Lord Can Grande della Scala, Vicar General of the Principate of the town of Verona and the municipality of Vicenza, his most devoted Dante Alighieri, Florentine in birth, sends his salutation." This greeting was more elegant than the ones Ser Dante had asked me to write for him, in simpler letters to his writer friends and his sons. I would have to practice if I were to help him with letters like this to important people, but after tricking the robbers I was sure I could conquer anything.

"I will read this in my chamber," he continued, "but your arrival is fortuitous. I have heard news only yesterday that Signor Dante's sons Giovanni, Pietro, and Iacopo are now allowed to travel to find their father. They are on their way north from their temporary home in the Casentino and can meet with him safely in Mantua, on the road to Padua, where they have been told their father is headed to see the new frescoes painted by his friend Giotto. I have arranged for the Alighieri sons to be accommodated at the palace of the Gonzaga rulers in Mantua, which will be a convenient stopping place for your master between Parma and Padua. The sons should reach Mantua in a few days. If you can return to your master in Parma quickly, both of you will reach

Mantua at about the same time. His sons must return to Florence after a short visit, but you and Dante can travel on to Padua."

My face shone with excitement. Giovanni and Pietro and Iacopo coming north to see us? In a safe place, under the supervision of Can Grande? My master would not be able to believe his good fortune.

That very afternoon I sped south to tell Ser Dante the good news. This time I never stopped to rest, reaching Parma in a day and a half. I was eager to tell him of my adventure with the *ladri*. "You did well, my son," he said. "You know how to get out of trouble when it befalls you. *Che fortunato* that they harmed neither you nor Gagliardo."

The next morning I saddled both the animals and replenished our supplies. Ser Dante and I hurried off again, this time to meet with Giovanni, Pietro, and Iacopo in Mantua.

On the way there, Ser Dante and I talked of the coming reunion. "My sons will be so tall that I will no longer think them children. How is it that they are free to come to me?"

"Signor Can Grande can explain," I said. "But the grooms in the stable told me that your poetry is being read in all the great courts and cities in the northern parts of Italy, so that Florentine enemies dare not enforce the threats to your family. You are becoming so famous, they say, that to harm your sons would be dangerous for them."

"*Ahi*! But are the Ghibellines still in power in Florence?"

"*Sì*. The death warrant for you, should you return, is still in place. But perhaps you could bargain with them?"

"If they wish me to renounce my beliefs and my allegiances, I shall never give in. But to see my boys will be joyful."

As we rode through the flat countryside and the marshy valleys along the Po River, Ser Dante told me more about the city to which we were headed.

"I hold Mantua in special esteem," he said, "because it was the home city of my favorite Roman poet, Virgil. He lived almost fourteen hundred years ago, and he wrote a long poem called the *Aeneid*, about the founding of Rome. In my poem, the *Commedia*, I use Virgil as my guide through the underworld."

"What does Virgil know about the underworld?"

"He wrote about it himself, in the *Aeneid*, because his hero Aeneas travels there to visit the spirit of his dead father."

"How does he get there?"

"In the south of Italy, on the western coast, there is a foul-smelling lake called

Avernus, and next to it a gloomy cave. That is the entrance." I shivered at the thought of diving into such a lake. "The ghost of Virgil appears in my poem," he continued:

Someone appeared before me whose voice
from long silence seemed faint.

'Have pity on me!' I cried to him,
'whoever you are, whether a shade or a real man.'

He answered, 'not a man now,
a man once I was, and both my parents
were Lombards, Mantuans by city,

and I lived in Rome under the good Augustus
at the time of the false and lying gods'.

"Why do you call the old gods 'false and lying,' Master?"

"Because at the time of the Roman Empire people believed in several gods, but many people now believe there is only one."

I thought about this. When I had gone to church with *Zia* Bianca, she had told me of someone called Jesus, who was the son of God. But I had never understood what a god was, and how a god could have a son. It seemed to me that having many gods might be sensible, because if you needed rain you could ask the rain god, or if you wanted to win in battle you could ask the war god to help you. Ser Dante kept on talking, partly to me and partly to himself.

"Some kind of force that we cannot see, but that we can call God if we want, helps us to lead better lives," he said. "We all make mistakes but we can learn and be forgiven." Thinking about all this made my head swim, like the night when we looked at the stars at Camaldoli and Ser Dante told me about the signs of the zodiac.

"Talking about such big ideas makes me feel warm and comfortable even though I don't understand it all. I like talking and traveling with you, Ser Dante. But tell me more about Virgil. Why is he so important to your poem if he lived so long ago?"

"Partly because he was such a great poet and I want to write as well as he. And partly because, being Roman, he stands for reason and logic. To understand the world you need both logic, about things you can see and prove, and faith, about things you believe in but which you can't see or prove."

I began to realize why traveling through Mantua, the home of Virgil, was so important to my master. Maybe the aura of the old poet would still be hanging over the city, and would breathe new inspiration into him.

CHAPTER TWENTY-SIX

WE crossed the Po, wide and wandering now, and reached the smaller stream called the Mincio encircling Mantua. The countryside was idyllic in October. The autumn air hung heavy with the thick sweet smells of fall, as vintners filled casks with wine and farmers harvested acorns from trees whose leaves flashed tinges of gold and coral. Several groups of strong workmen swung heavy clubs on branches of the oak trees, loosening the acorns so they would fall to the ground. Pigs foraged nearby. The more acorns they could find to eat, the fatter and healthier they would be. When these hogs were slaughtered and the meat cured for *prosciutto*, the *Mantovani* enjoying their fall winter meals would be fatter and healthier as well.

"These pig-fatteners look just like the ones carved on the cathedrals in Verona and Lucca," Ser Dante said. "In my poem I will claim that even the saints fatten pigs in the fall":

On this . . . St. Anthony fattens his pig
and others, too.

Nearby, other farm workers pressed the rich juice from the bursting grapes and poured it into casks to begin the fermentation of wine making. Seeing the fall wine-making activities reminded Ser Dante that our presence in Mantua this October was part of an ongoing cycle of enjoying the fruits of the past while preparing for pleasure and sustenance in the future. Thinking about this idea made me feel safe and comfortable.

"Are we tiny dots in a larger system?" I asked.

"Yes, if we look at life from a cosmic vantage point."

"What do you mean?"

"The cosmos is huge, bigger than the earth and the sky. What we see here are farmers and pigs, but from higher up they would look like specks, and the whole Po valley would look like an anthill, and the whole Italian peninsula would look like a crooked green bean. Imagine, Benito, if from the farthest vantage point we could even see different points in time, then we could see summer developing into fall and then on into spring and summer again. Human work fits into a grand design, especially if we help one another."

While I was trying to visualize Ser Dante's large ideas, I saw three figures approaching. They looked familiar and yet different. "Ser Dante! I think I see Giovanni, Pietro, and Iacopo! Look, they are running to meet us!" We dug our heels into Beffa and Galo and galloped ahead, stopping in a cloud of dust and leaping down to the road when the three Alighieri boys reached us. Their smiles were so big that their faces seemed all open mouths and teeth.

"*Dio vi benedica!* God bless you!" Ser Dante exclaimed, his eyes filling with tears. His arms folded around the boys and held them close. Iacopo untangled himself first, noticing me at last.

"Benito, can it be you? You have grown so tall!" He threw his arms around me in a bear hug so tight I could scarcely breathe.

"Yes, and so have you!" I said, slapping the shoulders of all three of them with my free hand. Even though Iacopo was as tall as his father, Ser Dante hoisted him up on Galo's back, and all of us walked into Mantua talking nonstop of old times in Florence. I had not seen Ser Dante so happy since he had told me about his love for Beatrice many years ago.

Luigi Gonzaga, prince of the Gonzaga family in Mantua, welcomed us warmly, and invited me to sleep with the Alighieri sons instead of with the stableboys. Ser Dante talked with them about his wife Gemma, his daughter Antonia, his half-brother Francesco, and his sisters. Francesco still worked the Alighieri family farms, but the sisters had drifted away, making new families of their own. First he asked about Gemma. Was she in good health, and not too lonely? Did she speak about him, and miss him? How about Antonia? Was she learning to read like her brothers? Was she happy? Then he asked about the fortunes of the lands in the Pagnolle. Were the tenant farmers paying their rents on time? Did their mother have enough *soldi* to pay the bills? Was their house still standing? How about the Ghibellines? Was there any chance that Ser Dante might return?

We feasted with Luigi and his courtiers, who bowed low to Ser Dante and told him in hushed tones how much they had heard about his poem, and how all the educated people at courts throughout the north of Italy were talking of it. Scribes were making copies and messengers were delivering them as fast as they could. The Mantuan court was sympathetic to the Guelphs, but gossip suggested that even the courts ruled by Ghibellines did not dare enforce the threats on Ser Dante's life or on the lives of his sons. His supporters were too many and his fame too great.

As I was preparing Ser Dante's belongings at bedtime, I asked, "Does this news mean you can return to Florence, and I to the Casentino?"

His shoulders stiffened. "No, I can never return. The Ghibellines will allow me back in Florence only if I sign a paper admitting my guilt, and since I am not guilty I shall never sign it. To ask me to do this is a bribe, and wrong. I can never agree to such a demand."

The few days in Mantua passed too quickly. Giovanni, Pietro, and Iacopo were almost hoarse from talking, but elated at meeting with their father at long last. As they prepared to return to their family's lands in Pagnolle, they assured their father that they would write often and would visit again whenever such a meeting became possible. He hugged them tightly and blessed them, telling them he counted on them to be responsible adults to care for their mother, their sister, and the family's possessions during his absence. On the morning they departed, he stayed in his quarters, unable to say *arrivederci* without tears.

Our next destination was Padua, across the Adige River and farther north in the Po River plain. Ser Dante seemed quiet and sad, being alone with me once again. After a day's traveling, however, his spirits brightened as he told me about his friend, the Tuscan painter Giotto, who had recently completed frescoes on the walls of a chapel in Padua. "They say that the colors glow, and that Giotto has given his biblical figures astonishingly thick solid bodies, unlike the flat thin ones painted in the old days. In addition to this strong bodily presence, I hear that the backgrounds and painted architecture look real too, as if one could walk into the painting. I want to admire the paintings myself, since I too strive in my poetry to make people and places as real as possible."

"Where are the paintings?" I asked.

"They are in a double row in the small Scrovegni Chapel, attached to the new palace rising on the grounds where the old Roman arena once was."

"Why is it called 'Scrovegni'?"

"A wealthy businessman named Enrico Scrovegni wanted his palace to be a showplace, so he commissioned Giotto to paint scenes from the lives of Jesus and his mother Mary in his private chapel. Some people say Enrico wanted to make the chapel particularly beautiful to make up for the evil done by his father, a banker who overcharged his clients, but his motives may be less important than the resulting spectacular art. Friends in Florence told me about Giotto's genius, and about how he has surpassed the earlier painters like Cimabue. I have written some lines:"

Cimabue was thought to hold the field in painting,
and now Giotto has the acclaim,
so that the other's fame is dim.

"But master, if artists learn to paint more realistically all the time, won't there be a new painter who will be better than Giotto before long?"

"Anyone who creates a work of art, whether it be painting or poetry or music, hopes that his creation will stand the test of time. But all too often the answer to your question is yes. I have written about that too:"

Worldly fame is nothing but a breath of wind,
which moves this way and that,
and changes name when it changes its direction.

"So the father of Enrico Scrovegni was greedy. But isn't the son a little greedy too, since he wanted to be proud of a costly painted display in his chapel?"

"You think well, and that is a difficult question. We must hope that, if the end results of such prideful artistic commissions are lovely paintings about subjects honoring God, who could object? I criticize evildoers in my poem, but I also want the readers to applaud my art describing how they atone for their sins. In any case, Giotto is truly a genius."

"Tell me about him."

"His real name was Ambrogio Bondone, and he was born a year after me, in 1266, in a little town near Florence named Vespignano. His father was a farmer. Stories about the young Giotto say that as he tended his father's flock he sketched the sheep on flat rocks in the pasture, so painting must have been in his blood. I knew him when we were boys in Florence. Later he painted frescoes about the life of *San Francesco*, Saint Francis, in Assisi."

We kept moving toward the northeast, crossed the Adige, and at last reached the crowded noisy streets of the city of Padua. Wandering through the maze of crooked pathways, we dodged the rough-wheeled carts bouncing over the cobblestones and asked directions from the shopkeepers and merchants busy selling wine, nuts, and cheese.

"It is exciting to be back in a city, but I miss the quiet of the river flatlands," I said.

"We need both," Ser Dante replied. "Life would be boring if it were always the same."

"I know something else we need," I said. "*Colazione*, lunch. I smell marvelous odors coming from cookpots, and my stomach is growling."

Ser Dante bargained for some grilled river trout and a bit of bread and wine, and we sat down to eat. The combination of our hunger and the savory fish hid some other less pleasant smells wafting up from some nearby garbage pens under the overhanging balconies.

"Let's go on," I said. "The chapel must be in a part of town smelling nicer than this."

When we reached the small piazza abutting the chapel we found others, like ourselves, eager to enter. Inside, it was easy to lose oneself in the painted story-telling world of the luminous frescoes. One in particular caught my eye, halfway down the left on the lower level. It portrayed a sweep of barren rock, and at the bottom left the heavy body of Christ being held by his mother and others. "What do you call this scene?" I asked.

"It is called the *Lamentation.* Can you feel the love, as well as the sorrow? Giotto painted the haloes of Christ and his mother as interlocking, forming one solid compassionate unit. Look at the stubby angels in the sky...can't you almost hear them wailing? The dramatic foreshortening makes them look as if they could fly right out over our heads."

"It is sad but happy at the same time," I said.

"You and I have been both sad and happy too," Ser Dante replied, "sad to leave Florence but happy to have the opportunity to travel, to write, and to make new friends. I think Giotto and I are on similar missions, to teach and to comfort others." We passed by other scenes, marveling at the brilliant blues, reds, and golds.

"Being in here is like listening to the chanting music at Sant'Antimo," I said. "Being inside a church and soaking up art warm me."

Ser Dante stood quietly, surrounded by the colored images. "Art can cure and comfort," he said. "I must continue to make my poem as moving as I can, like Giotto's paintings. If I succeed my life will have been worthwhile despite our misfortunes. Padua has been well worth the journey."

CHAPTER TWENTY-SEVEN

WE settled in Padua for Ser Dante to work on his manuscript, now nearing completion. It was here that Ser Dante gave me a second big chance at being a courier. I was to travel alone to Venice, to deliver copies of his poem to members of the Great Council ruled by the Doge. I had heard travelers' tales of the city, a rich trading port on the Adriatic coast with watery canals instead of streets. I could hardly believe my ears when Ser Dante asked me to travel there, because Venice sounded like a fable instead of a real place.

"What is a doge?" I asked.

"He is the governor of the city, and since Venice is a republic, he is duly elected by the people. The Great Council to which you will deliver my papers is largely made up of the important Venetian families, whose representatives select the leader—the word *doge* comes from the Latin word for leader, *dux*. It's a forward-looking independent city, called *La Serenissima*, the most peaceful."

"Is it really built on water?"

"*Sì*, it is made up of more than a hundred little islands and lagoons, where the early settlers moved hundreds of years ago to protect themselves from attack. Their skill at ship-building made them indispensable to rulers far across the ocean to the east."

The idea of traveling across the ocean in fast Venetian ships sent a thrill through me. "Were they ever attacked by pirates?"

"Often. But they were so strong and so clever that they defeated the pirates, making the seas safer for travel and for trade. People call Venice the 'bride of the sea.'"

"Why?"

"Venice exists hand in hand with the sea, and depends on its riches for her livelihood. In May there is a festival, the *Festa della Sensa*, symbolizing the marriage. At that time the Doge dresses in gold and travels out in the lagoon on his golden vessel, the *Bucintoro*. As he throws a golden wedding ring into the sea, he says 'We wed you, o Sea, as a sign of true and perpetual dominion.'"

"Why is Venice so rich with gold?"

"The Venetians controlled trade between the east and the west, bringing silks and spices and gold for marketing in their city. When you enter the main square, the *Piazza San Marco*, you will see above its entrance to the great basilica four great bronze horses, brought back by the Venetians when crusaders conquered the eastern city of Constantinople."

My eyes widened. Going to Venice was going to be my greatest adventure yet, one I could never have imagined on *Zia* Bianca's farm in the Casentino. This time I was going to keep close watch on Galo and keep my wits about me. I would be worthy of Ser Dante's trust.

It was November by the time Galo and I made our way eastward along the banks of a stream. I watched farmhands corralling the last stray pigs toward their winter pens, while they pulled the last turnips from the fields and collected the last acorns from the trees. Years of working outdoors had tanned and creased their skins and sculpted their arms and legs into powerful muscles. Keeping the hogs in a steadily moving stream required most of their attention, but I heard a greeting now and then. "*Olà*!" they called, "where are you headed?"

"To Venice," I said. "Is this the shortest way?"

"*Certo*," they replied. "Follow this creek till it turns into wetlands near the ocean. There, you will find boatmen who will ferry you out to Venice for a few *soldi*." Once, when a group of field hands were taking a short break to eat some *biscotti* from their knapsacks, I stopped to eat and talk with them.

"Is Venice as rich and golden as people say?" I asked.

They chuckled. "Some parts are, but most of it is dirty and crowded like any other city. Except you will travel on muddy water instead of on a muddy street."

They were right about the swamplands near the coast. Galo sank up to his knees in the muck. Ahead of me and across a pebbled inlet, I saw two flat-bottomed skiffs tied to a dock. Behind the dock was a fenced corral on higher ground. A fellow seated on the dock spotted me, jumped into one of the boats, and paddled near. "Back your horse up to the rise on your left," he said, "he will only sink further into the mud if you go forward." Galo was nervous, but I managed to pull up the reins and edge him backward, a step at a time. "*Bene*," the man said. "I will open the gate and you can tether him in the pasture with the other two horses you see there."

The man seemed honest, but thoughts of the *briganti* near Peschiera flashed across my mind. Perhaps he was trying to steal Galo from me. "*Signore*, I am trying to go to Venice to deliver some important messages. How can I get there with my horse?"

"Ah, you must be *un uomo di campagna*, a man of the land, rather than *un uomo di mare*, a man of the sea. One cannot take a horse into Venice." I was glad he had called me a man, but worried at the prospect of having to leave Galo in someone else's care. "You see that chestnut mare behind the fence? I am keeping her for Signor Can Grande of Verona, who is visiting in Venice. I can keep your horse also, if you come back with some fresh caught eels and octopus for me on your way back."

"So you know Can Grande? He is my friend, to whom I have just delivered some letters from my master."

"*Certo*. Can Grande is a good man and a good ruler, and he knows I take good care of horses. You can leave yours here too. My name is Alberto. Since it is nearly December I will put extra hay in the feed bins and cover the horses with blankets at night. They will be happy here." His words convinced me.

"How do I get to Venice, then?"

"In my little boat here, the *Marco Polo*. I ferry you out and you tell me when you wish me to return to bring you back."

On the ride over, I asked Alberto why he had named his boat the *Marco Polo*.

"Our proud city, *La Serenissima,* was the home of the explorer Marco Polo. He set out for the east from Venice about the time I was born, and reached what he called China and India after difficult travels through seas, deserts, and mountains. I figure if *he* could get that far, my little dinghy would do well to be named after him."

"What did he find there?" I asked. China and India seemed ever so much farther away than Lucca or Parma or even Rome.

"When they put him in prison in Genoa he wrote a book about it, but I don't believe everything he said."

"Why?"

"Well, he says he stayed at the court of the great Kublai Khan, and he tells big stories about gold, jade, porcelain, silk, ivory, and spices. I never learned to read, but Can Grande told me some people call the book *Il Milione*, the million, because in it Marco Polo speaks of the million riches of the Asian kings. Me, I call it *Il Milione* because it sounds like a million lies."

Venice was sounding more and more exciting. A floating city filled with gold and spices, along with a lot of mud and travelers telling exotic stories. I couldn't wait to get there.

Once we moved out of the marshes, the sparkling water reflected the bright winter sunlight like twinkling stars around the boat. After a gently rocking ride, we reached a *banchina* or quay where Alberto tied up the *Marco Polo*. Above me I saw two tall columns topped with carvings. Alberto told me they were the symbols of the city, the winged lion of Saint Mark and the figure of Saint Theodore.

"Saint Theodore was the original patron saint of Venice," he said, "before the bones of the current patron saint, Saint Mark, were rescued in Egypt and brought back to Venice around five hundred years ago. We Venetians are proud of our brave founders." Returning to the business at hand, he said, "I will return for you tomorrow at noon, and don't forget the octopus. My wife makes a delicious *zuppa di pesce*, fish stew, but only when she can get fresh *frutti di mare,* seafood, from the lagoon."

Fishermen were everywhere, and the first odors accosting my nose were pungent. "Buy from me! Fresh grilled swordfish and shrimp! They leapt from the sea into my pan!" called a vendor. I bought a few shrimp, licking my lips at the delicate flesh, and began walking. The city was a maze of canals cluttered with boats of all shapes and sizes, bridges, and narrow passageways between buildings.

I asked a passerby how to get to the meeting place of the Great Council, and he waved me toward the magnificent domes of the *Basilica di San Marco*, where I saw the great bronze horses Ser Dante had mentioned. They were prancing as if they would jump right off the roof and down into the *piazza* below. "The Great Council meets there, in the building to the right called the *Palazzo Ducale,* the Doge's Palace," he said. Thanking him, I entered and presented Ser Dante's correspondence to the *segretario particolare*. He, as private secretary to the Doge, assured me of the letter's delivery. My duties completed, I returned to the spacious piazza, where I heard a familiar voice.

"Benito, what brings you to Venice?" Spinning around, I was overjoyed to see Can Grande himself. "I can't believe my good fortune at finding you here," he said, "I have a letter for your master Dante of great importance, just given to me by a courier from Ravenna. It contains news of a prized invitation."

"*Che fortunato*!" I said. "I will deliver it to him tomorrow when I return with Alberto, who is keeping my horse along with yours."

"Alberto is coming for me tomorrow too," Can Grande said. "Come, we have time to admire the carvings on the basilica before finding a place to eat and sleep tonight."

Around the central doorway were concentric circles with figures showing the labors of the months, along with twisted scrolls of plants, sea birds, and the signs of the zodiac. The November figure was trying to catch water birds, an activity well suited to Venice. On the next circle carvers had represented typically Venetian trades, like fishing and boat building.

"Can Grande, you first introduced me to looking at carvings like this, back in Verona. We had so much fun talking and playing, do you remember?"

"Of course. The longer I live, and especially now as I try to govern Verona justly and fairly, I see that there is a rhythm to our Italian lives. Do you know what sort of work many of the Venetians do during the winter? I can show you at the shipyards, where workers are mending sails, caulking hulls, and making ropes."

"So," I replied, "profitable work can be done in the fields or in the city—or even anywhere, if it is governing, the work that you do, or writing, the work that Ser Dante does."

"Have you thought, Benito, about what sort of work you want to do, once you are finished with service for Dante?"

"I have learned to write, and I like composing and delivering letters. Perhaps I will hire myself out as a courier."

"*Magnifico*! I am in need of a courier myself, so when Ser Dante no longer needs you, come back to Verona and work with me."

My face glowed with delight. My services were needed, and by a great lord! Tomorrow we would both return, I to Padua and Can Grande to Verona. Ser Dante would be proud of me. I had delivered his message safely and Can Grande had offered me a courier position in the Scaligeri court. The important letter from Ravenna was safe in my pocket, to give to Ser Dante. Can Grande had said it contained an important invitation. What could this be?

CHAPTER TWENTY-EIGHT

SER Dante welcomed Galo and me back safely from our expedition to Venice, congratulated me on my good fortune—the future work with Can Grande—and before reading the letter from Ravenna insisted I tell him about the trip. He was always curious about how people lived, in various parts of Italy and at different times of year, and Venice was unique. As I talked with him I could see the words forming in his mind as he shaped ideas for his poem from my descriptions of winter activities in the port city:

> *in the shipyards of the Venetians,*
> *In winter, the tenacious pitch boils*
> *to caulk their damaged ships,*
>
> *since the sailors cannot navigate, and instead*
> *some build new boats, some strengthen the ribs*
> *of one that has made many voyages;*
>
> *some hammer at the prow and some at the stern;*
> *some make oars, and some twist ropes;*
> *some mend the jib and mainsail.*

"Just as their cousins in the mountains or the fields prepare the soil, plant, harvest, herd sheep, or make wine, the shipyard workers in Venice work at the backbone of their community's life too—in their case, sailing the Adriatic Sea," he said. "There is a place for many different contributions, and all of them work together to keep our society running well."

"That's true," I replied, although I grew a little impatient. "Can Grande said the message he was to deliver to you contained something important. Can you open it now?" I liked to hear him talk about art and life, but I wanted to know what the special invitation was.

I handed him the letter. He read it first to himself and then a second time aloud, so I could hear the news. The writer began with great praise. Ser Dante's face flushed upon reading the acclaim that was coming to him by readers of his long poem, the *Commedia*.

I interrupted him, bursting with curiosity about who the writer from Ravenna was. "Who sent this via Can Grande, Ser Dante? Tell me!"

"The letter is stamped with the great seal of the court of Ravenna, with an eagle symbolizing power," he said, "and it is from the hand of the lord of that city, Guido Novello da Polenta."

"What does he ask?"

"I will tell you," he replied. "He requests my presence at the court there, offering me a secure place in which to write in exchange for some small diplomatic duties writing and delivering court letters to neighboring cities. He says my fame is widespread and many thinkers want to come and talk with me. In fact, he refers to me as the *sommo poeta*, the greatest poet of our time. He wants me to make Ravenna my second home, as his guest there."

"Is Ravenna like Venice, with canals? I have heard that it is on the Adriatic coast too."

"Nothing is comparable to Venice, but you are right that Ravenna is also on the coast, farther south. The Polenta family has long ruled there. Eight hundred years ago, after the city of Rome was invaded by barbarians, Ravenna became the head of the Roman Empire. It is a cultured city, with beautiful churches decorated with mosaics. I will be honored to reside there. Guido da Polenta says that my wife and children can join me to live at his court."

"What wonderful news! I am happy for you, Ser Dante. Who is Guido da Polenta?"

"He is a good and compassionate ruler, and he appreciates poetry. He wants to allow me time to write in warmth, peace, and quiet. When I was not busy writing, he says I would be free to mingle and talk with other intellectuals and writers gathered at his court."

"Even when I am working in Verona, I will certainly have to travel to Ravenna from time to time," I said. I did not like to think yet about the end of my travels with Ser Dante, despite the exciting prospects of my new work with Can Grande.

"You will always be welcome." he replied, "as one of my family." My eyes filled with tears. Ser Dante truly thought of me now as a son. Turning back to thoughts of his writing, he told me that he would include praise for Guido in his poem, to thank him for his welcome and his hospitality:

Ravenna stands as it has for many years,
the eagle of Polenta brooding over it.

"I will travel with you to Ravenna and make sure you are comfortably situated," I said, "before taking my leave to join the court of Can Grande."

My head spun with thoughts of completing my work with Ser Dante and starting off on my own. For now, however, I busied myself with plans for our winter journey.

Ravenna lay directly south of Venice. I had not traveled in this part of Italy, so I questioned Ser Dante about the terrain.

"In warmer weather," he said, "boat travel in the shallow marshlands between Venice and Ravenna would be easy. But since we are now into December, any transportation will be difficult. Winds roll down to the sea from the mountains, bringing with them a dusting of frost and a coating of crackling ice on the marshes. If one travels far enough from shore, a flat-bottomed boat might be the easiest and quickest means of transport, avoiding the need to climb farther inland where the deltas of the Po and the Adige Rivers slope upward and winters are harsher. One has to choose between the partially frozen delta and the icy mountain slopes."

"Which will be better for us?"

"If we hire a boat strong enough to cut through small ice patches, and if we stay outside the marshy waterways and travel primarily in the shallow Adriatic surf, we could reach Ravenna in several days. I will send you to look for such a boat and boatman."

I saddled Galo again and retraced my steps back toward the coastline, this time avoiding the mud at the edge of the marshes. My new friend Alberto directed me to a fisherman going south, and from him I secured winter transport between the Venetian coast and Ravenna for Ser Dante and myself.

"*Bene,*" Ser Dante said when I returned. We left Galo and Beffa in Padua with friends of Can Grande, with my promise to collect the animals on my return, on my way to Verona. My master kept his letter from Guido safe, wrapped in the folds of his heavy woolen tunic, when we boarded the small wooden craft. His strength was not equal to what it had been as we began our travels, and I knew he would be shivering on the sea journey. Still, choosing that route was the best option.

Midwinter was a time best suited to staying indoors, as bears did when they hibernated in dark warm dens. In a city like Venice, winter was a time to stay inside and repair tools and boats. Ser Dante saw beauty in winter:

our air sends down flakes
of snow in winter when the horn
of Capricorn is touched by the sun.

But he knew all too well that it could also be devastating. Toward the end of his *Inferno*, the gravest sinners of all—the traitors—suffered from a cold so intense they could no longer see through their frozen eyes and could never feel the warmth of heaven:

Their eyes, which previously were wet only within,
gushed through their lids, and the cold
froze their tears and locked them up again.

A clamp never bound wood to wood so strongly.

The letter from Guido da Polenta had come at an opportune time. Ser Dante's poem was nearly done. Ravenna would be an ideal place for him to settle and complete his work. "I will be happy there," he said, "with love and care from my family and with the friendship and conversation of Italy's wise thinkers."

CHAPTER TWENTY-NINE

GUIDO da Polenta welcomed us cordially, ushering Ser Dante into a quiet airy study. He dictated his first letter to me and sent it off by courier to Can Grande de la Scala soon after we arrived, despite fatigue from the journey. Thanking his patron profusely, both for his past kindnesses and for offering me service at his court, Ser Dante honored his long-time friend in Verona by informing him that he intended to dedicate the last section of his poem—the *Paradiso*—to Can Grande.

Writing the letter also offered Ser Dante the opportunity to put into more precise words the structure and over-arching themes of his poem. He dictated it to me, detailing the purpose, divisions, and levels of the poem.

In the first section, the *Inferno*, he had imagined himself as both the writer and the traveler. Attempting to find the way to truth, he made his way down into hell, which he imagined as a cone-shaped crater spiraling downward toward the center of the earth. In nine circles, becoming smaller and more crowded as he descended, he saw sinners who had committed grave crimes, with the worst offenders at the bottom. At the earth's icy center he turned his head where his feet had been and climbed back up to the earth's surface, where he would see the mountain of *Purgatorio*. Traveling through this mountain comprised the second major section of the poem. Here, criminals who repented could work off their sins and gradually rise to *Paradiso*, the poem's final section. He told Can Grande that he had peopled all three sections with true-to-life Italian acquaintances, including enemies as well as friends. By the poem's end, Dante the writer and Dante the traveler—both poet and pilgrim—had grown both wiser and humbler, enlightened by their experiences. The traveler had reached salvation, and his journey could represent the journey of every person moving through life.

"Ser Dante, when I work for Can Grande I will tell everyone about your magnificent poem," I said. "And I will keep reading it myself, understanding more and more of its deeper significance."

"Here is something you can easily comprehend," he said. "In the *Paradiso* I have written in the voice of my great-great-grandfather Cacciaguida, who like me praises Can Grande. Here is what Cacciaguida says about Can Grande:"

His liberality will be known,

so that even his enemies
will not keep silent about him.

Count on him and on his benefits;
through him the fate of many will be transformed,
rich and poor changing places.

I recognized myself as one of those among the poor whose fate had been changed by my experiences with Ser Dante and with Can Grande. How fortunate I was!

Guido, like Can Grande, was a bountiful host. He ruled a city resplendent with churches decorated with shimmering mosaics. Ser Dante made sure I visited the church of San Vitale to see the glittering presentations on its walls of the emperor Justinian and his empress Theodora. "In these Christian mosaics Theodora appears as an aristocratic and elegant woman with dangling earrings. She was a cabaret dancer before she married the Roman emperor."

"Everyone has a place in churches! When painters and sculptors show ordinary people as well as scenes from the Bible, all of us are drawn in."

"The combination you describe is what I try to do in my writing too. Justinian wasn't a religious figure, but he was a good ruler, establishing a fair code of laws. Here is what I wrote about him:"

I am Justinian
who, through the will of the Holy Spirit,
removed from the laws what was superfluous and vain.

"It is fitting that our host Guido is lord over Ravenna," Ser Dante commented. "He loves these beautiful mosaics and he has studied history too. All good rulers need to have a fascination for ideas. His study has made him peace loving and generous, and he distributes his wealth sensibly, to help where it is needed. Like Can Grande, his government is stable and he rules with Christian goodness. You and I are in good hands."

"His rule reminds me of Siena, where the Lorenzetti brothers were planning their fresco for the city hall. Their goal was to educate the Sienese about good and bad government through pictures on the walls."

"If the Florentines had understood messages like that, you and I would not be exiled. But in some ways exile has become a good thing for both of us. We have gained friends and knowledge, and we have been welcomed in compassionate courts. Good government means that besides being good citizens themselves, individuals must put the welfare of the community above their own individual desires. It also means that hard work brings prosperity and enjoyment for everyone." Ser Dante's words sank into my consciousness. I hoped I too had learned to put others' needs ahead of my own.

Through Guido's generosity Dante's wife Gemma and his children did come to Ravenna as guests of the ruler. Giovanni, Pietro, and Iacopo had grown even taller since I had seen them in Mantua. I was glad that Antonia came too. She was beautiful and accomplished. Her brothers had taught her at home much of what they learned in school, since girls didn't have the benefit of schooling. Pietro had learned to work with his uncle Francesco, the sibling remaining closest to Dante, supervising the family farms in the Casentino. "Your *Zia* Bianca sends her love," Pietro told me. "She is older now, but her children care for her well. They till her land, and crops are thriving. She misses you but is happy you have met with such good fortune. As a present for you, she sent these ripe melons from the farm with us. They made big lumps in our saddlebags, but they had to be delivered to you!"

Antonia particularly enjoyed the time with the Polenta family. Since she hadn't been allowed to travel with her brothers to see her father in Mantua, the time they spent together was especially dear. During their long talks in the evenings, she told him about her desire to join a cloistered religious order, telling him that she wanted more than anything to become a nun, praising God and helping others. Of course her father agreed. She went to the cloister with Ser Dante's love and blessings, and we all promised to visit her often. Ser Dante was honored when she took the convent name of Beatrice, the woman who had inspired his poetry.

The Ravenna court became for Ser Dante a Florence-in-exile, where his friends and family could gather, clustering about him like birds warming each other in winter. Some came and then returned home, and others traveled to Ravenna to stay. Ser Dante wrote of this comparison:

as by natural custom, the daws move together
at the beginning of the day
to warm their cold feathers,

then some go away without returning,
others fly back to where they started,
and still others delay, circling about.

Ser Dante himself managed some occasional travel too, to deliver Guido's diplomatic messages. I would be leaving soon, but his sons and other young members of the Ravenna court would be able assistants to him for such journeys. My last days with Ser Dante were bittersweet. He had become like a father to me, but it was time now for me to try my own wings. To avoid too much heartache, I concentrated on the daily routines at the Polenta court rather than on my imminent departure.

Ser Dante rose early, writing every morning until well after midday. Settling himself in the comfortable leather and wood chair Guido had provided, he picked up his quill pen and transported himself into the paradise of his poem. Shortly after noon Guido would send a court messenger, bringing a plate of bread, cheeses, and fruit and a small bottle of the local white wine, sometimes a Soave that Can Grande sent down from Verona or sometimes a Vernaccia from Tuscany. Gemma, his children and I would join him for a simple *pranzo*, meal, and a time of rest. By late afternoon he was back at his desk, either engaged in diplomatic correspondence or plunging once again into his great poem.

We left him alone when he was writing. I had been with him for so long that I could surmise what he was thinking about, even though his family did not fully understand what he was writing. It was true that despite the poem being peopled with everyday Italians, its goals were complex. I loved reading some of the wild descriptions, but even I didn't always know what they meant. Pietro and Iacopo found it hard to believe that their father truly thought he had traveled to Hell, Purgatory, and Paradise, and had returned to write of his journey. Even so, they began to see the story through their father's eyes and heart, and to realize that the poem had many levels. It was a happy time for all of us, because we all loved Ser Dante and treated him with respect. It was a great honor for him and his family that he was revered at the court of Ravenna.

Evenings were spent enjoying Guido's courtly suppers. His cooks often served the *risotto* and seafood loved in the region, and dinners were accompanied by the crusty flat bread Ser Dante had learned to like, even if he never forgot the unsalted bread of his native Florence. He enjoyed witty conversations with well traveled and knowledgeable guests, who came to hear him read the latest verses in his poem. From them he learned about political and literary activities in all of northern Italy.

Ser Dante was happy and well cared for, and I had given him all I could. As March came around once again, the Polenta family planned a special celebration for my sixteenth birthday. The *capocuoco* made a *risotto* with *granchi*, sea crabs, and baked a special *panettone* for me, a cakebread with raisins and dried fruits. After dinner Ser Dante sat in a wide armchair in the grand salon and we all listened while he read to us the latest verses in his poem. In the poem I recognized people, places, and experiences that we had shared. My eyes misted over as I remembered all the travels we had been through together. He had taught me to take care of myself and to be brave, and we had been good company for each other for many years. A tiny voice inside me hoped that he had learned a few things from me too.

Later in the evening, after Gemma and his children had gone to bed, I sat alone with him, wondering how I could express my thoughts. As I pondered what to say, my words drew strength from our years of travel and conversation. "Ser Dante," I said finally, "you have shaped me into the kind of young man I hoped to be. When I meet challenges I will think of you, and how you always face danger with dignity and bravery. I have learned from you the most important lessons of my life, about caring for other people's feelings and making sure everyone is treated fairly. I have learned to recognize good and evil, and to try to embrace the good. I have learned to be happy with what I have and not to grieve over what I lack. I have learned to love beauty, whether in the countryside, people, animals, poetry, art, or music. I have learned to respect all the hard working Italians who have treated us so warmly. How can I ever thank you enough?"

He turned to look at me, his eyes overflowing with tears. "You have been my best friend, Benito. I love you very much, and you go to Can Grande with my blessings. *Pace e bene*, peace and good will."

I was weeping too, as I hugged him. "I love you too, Ser Dante. The world will be a better place because of you."

"I want you to take Galo with you. He has grown to love you, and you will need a swift horse to carry messages for the court of Verona. Beffa can stay with me to take care of my needs."

"*Mille grazie,* Ser Dante. I will never forget you."

Before I went to bed I slipped quietly into the stable to say goodbye to Beffa. The next morning I packed my few things, saddled Galo, and set off for Verona.

CHAPTER THIRTY

I worked at the court of Can Grande in Verona for more than twelve years, writing and delivering diplomatic letters to courts throughout northern Italy. Traveling to many cities including Venice, Ferrara, Parma, Arezzo, Borgo San Donnino, Cremona, Mantua, and Ravenna, I met many wise people and marveled at many art works, especially those about the earthly labors Ser Dante so loved. I gained the confidence of many rulers and courtiers, composing in the careful language I had learned from him and maintaining the respect he always showed for others. One afternoon in mid-September of the year 1321 Can Grande called me into his private study.

"Benito," he said, "I have some sad news for you. A courier has come to Verona today to tell us that our beloved Dante is now in his own paradise, as he described in his poem the *Commedia*. He died at peace with the world."

I stiffened. We both knew that Dante, like everyone else, was mortal. But I never expected his death. I had never really believed he would ever die. Tears came to my eyes, and I saw Can Grande was crying too. Ser Dante was part of my life, and the thought of not having him was like losing my arm. "Oh, Can Grande," I said, "we will mourn him together." Then I couldn't form any more words, and we hugged each other and wept.

When we regained our composure, Can Grande spoke. "You must know that Dante completed his poem, the *Commedia*, but I doubt you have read the final verses. His vision of heaven in the *Paradiso* goes far beyond an imaginary journey through the afterlife. Somehow, spawned by our admiration of the carvings on the church of San Zeno, he has incorporated all his love for the work we Italians do throughout the year, season after season, into one great song of praise for human destiny. He sees the world written large, with all of us as segments of a larger plan. At the end of the poem he writes,"

the human image was conformed
to the divine circle and has a place in it.

"There will be an empty place in my heart for him, but he taught me well. In his verses there is always a warm kinship with the daily lives of Italians. What sustained them through autumn, winter, spring, and back to summer sustained him in his work as well. I think the *Commedia* tells their stories in cycles of nature, life, and the cosmos."

"At the end of the poem, he imagines a heavenly rose, pulsating with light and music. Listen:"

In the form of a white rose

like a swarm of bees, at times lighting
on a flower and then returning
to where their toil is turned to sweetness,

descended into the great flower
adorned with so many leaves, and then rose
to where their love always dwells.

They all had faces of living flames,
and golden wings, and the rest so white
that no snow equals the whiteness.

"It is beautiful," I said. "How does he end the poem?"

"The last lines of the *Paradiso*," he replied, "end with the word *stelle*, stars, like the last lines of the *Inferno* and the *Purgatorio*. Dante completed his vision by locating the source of love and perfection and truth in the heavens, like this:"

For the great imagination here power failed;
but already my desire and will, in harmony,

were turning like a wheel moved evenly

by the love which turns the sun and the other stars.

"How did he die?" I asked.

"Last spring, not too long after he had completed the *Paradiso*, an argument arose about two ships, one from Ravenna and one from Venice. After they collided in the Adriatic, the sailors on board engaged in fierce fighting, straining the relationship between the governments of the two cities. Guido da Polenta, fearing that greater hostilities would occur, pleaded with Dante to go as a peacemaker between the two seaport cities. Our great poet had made a name for himself as a wise thinker and writer, and especially as one who valued peaceful co-existence of all people throughout life's cycles, whether good or bad.

"Although his great poem was finished, he was still fully engrossed in literary life, exchanging poems with other writers and discussing ideas with friends. Realizing the need, however, for Ravenna's help in bringing about a peaceful solution to the maritime conflict, he accepted the task. Taking a short break from his writing and from the intellectual life of the court, he traveled north, reversing the boat trip he had made when you journeyed south with him years ago to join the Ravenna court. Through his skill at advocating mutual benefit and through his convincing oratory, he was instrumental in establishing a temporary peaceful settlement.

"To Guido's great relief, and also to the relief of the Venetian doge, the settlement was to be solidified at a second meeting the following September. This time Dante traveled part of the distance over land, through the salt marshes in the delta of the Po River. Fall had come early, and the nights brought chill winds, damp weather, and many *zanzare*, mosquitoes. His health, already weakened, was no match for the elements. He contracted malaria, a disease well known to all of us from its name itself, 'mal aria' or 'bad air.' Suffering from chills, headaches, and fatigue, he barely made his way home to Guido's court. The disease proved too much for him, and he died in Ravenna on the night of September thirteenth, at age fifty-six."

"Ser Dante gone," I whispered. "I cannot believe it."

"The day of his death coincided with the feast of the Exaltation of the Cross, a fitting parallel to the poet whose *Commedia* traces the progress of a pilgrim through sin and penitence and finally to redemption in heaven. His family and friends continue to grieve, along with Guido da Polenta. Mourners crowned his body with the laurel wreath worthy of a poet, and his coffin was carried to the church of San Francesco. It pains me to be the one to tell you, because of all the people he loved you were perhaps the closest to him."

Ser Dante had died doing what he believed in most—helping men and communities to get along well with one another. I would never forget him.

His bones themselves—like Dante in life—did not remain in one location but continued to journey. In 1519, nearly three hundred years after Dante's death, the Pope ordered the crypt opened so the bones could be removed and placed in a more grandiose tomb in Tuscany. The tomb was empty. Franciscan monks worried about the safety of his remains had taken them to a secret place. Once more, in 1677, the Franciscans had to repeat their move, to guarantee that Dante's remains would stay in Ravenna. After this removal, the location of the bones was not known until 1865, when they were found by workers involved in restoration work in a nearby church. Since then they have been safely enshrined in Ravenna, in a burial vault in the church of San Francesco.

Dante's dream of returning to Florence never left him, but remained only a dream. He never gave up wanting to go back to his home,

by the beautiful Arno river, in the great city.

In the *Paradiso* he voiced his desire hauntingly:

If it ever happens that the sacred poem
to which Heaven and earth have set hand,
and which has kept me lean for many years,

overcomes the cruelty which has barred me
from the fair sheepfold where, a lamb, I slept,
a foe to the wolves that war on it,

then with another voice and another fleece, a beard,
I will return a poet, and on the font
of my baptism I will receive the laurel crown;

At last Dante's wanderings were over. His life–like his poem–had come to completion.